**If everything's so great,
why do I feel so miserable?**

"We really miss you, you know," Julie told me as my friends trooped out the door of my hospital room.

For some reason hearing Julie say that almost made me cry, because it didn't really seem like my friends missed me very much at all. There they were, all excited about the party, planning their costumes and all the fun things they were going to do. It was obvious that they could do it perfectly well without me. And then there was Jennifer. For people who just a few days earlier hadn't felt comfortable even eating lunch with her, my friends seemed to be getting along with her just fine. *Maybe they'll want her to join The Party Line permanently,* I thought. *Maybe . . . maybe she'll take my place.*

Ask your bookseller for these other PARTY LINE titles:

Special party tips in every book!

ROSIE'S MYSTERY ON ICE

by Carrie Austen

SPLASH™

B

A BERKLEY / SPLASH BOOK

Rosie's Mystery on Ice

One

"Too juvenile."

"Too nerdy."

"Too expensive."

It was a Sunday afternoon, and my three best friends and I were sitting in Becky Bartlett's attic, trying to come up with a fabulous idea for Sarah Barrow's birthday party. The party was scheduled for that coming Saturday, and we had already decided it would be an ice-skating party. We wanted to come up with something that would give it real pizzaz, though.

It's not that we don't do a super job on every party we do. The Party Line—that's our party business—treats every job as if it were for the Queen of the Universe. And we don't just do fantastic parties—we make good money, too.

We've been in business for a while, doing parties mostly for young children. We've done fairytale parties, monster parties, dinosaur parties, roller-skating parties, you name it.

Besides, we wanted Sarah's party to be extra special. Not only is Sarah's older sister, Liz Barrow, one of our friends from school, but her older brother is Ben Barrow, one of the cutest guys on the planet.

We were practically short-circuiting our brains trying to come up with something completely def. *Def* as in *definitive*: the party to end all parties. (Well, not really. The end of all parties would also be the end of The Party Line! We just wanted it to be the greatest party we ever did—until we did the next one!)

Anyway, we were looking for a party that would put us on the map, so to speak. But as we sat there in the attic, it seemed like we were going nowhere fast. Every idea we came up with just wasn't quite right.

My very best friend, Julie Berger, munched thoughtfully on a pretzel. "There's got to be something that would be really great, really unique. I mean, the kids go ice skating all the time."

"True," said Becky. "Well, let's go over what we've got so far, okay?" Becky is the president of The Party Line, and she really does keep our meetings moving along. She makes sure we don't just goof off and eat junk food.

"Okay," said Julie, reaching for her notebook. Julie is the secretary, so she takes notes on all the things we discuss at the meetings. She has the best handwriting, and she's also the only person I know who can do just about anything and eat at the same time. Now Julie flipped through her notebook, crunching away. She swallowed and cleared her throat as if she were about to perform an opera or read Shakespeare or something.

"The party's going to be Saturday afternoon at the ice-skating rink in Van Fleet Park. There'll be about twenty fifth-graders."

Allie Gray pulled a sheet of paper from a folder in her lap. "Maybe I should run through what we know about Sarah first," she suggested. Allie is the vice president, and she's the one who keeps us organized. When we first started the business, Allie created an information sheet that we use to plan each party. Whoever gets called about a job fills one out, asking the client all sorts of questions about the birthday kid and what he or she likes.

"Read away," Becky told her.

"Sarah's going to be ten years old, she loves ice skating, and her mother says her favorite flavor is chocolate—in everything from cookies to candy to ice cream. Her favorite color is hot pink; she collects stuffed animals, especially rabbits; and her nickname is Fat Tuesday," Allie read.

"What?" Julie shouted.

Allie looked up, a little bewildered at the interruption. "Where should I go back to?" she asked. "Her nickname?"

"Of course, nimbo!" Julie was giggling so hard I thought she'd fall over. "What kind of nickname is Fat Tuesday?"

"One she hates, I bet," said Becky.

"I don't think she minds," Allie said. "Her mom said she even has a T-shirt personalized with her nickname, and she loves to wear it. She's really pretty, and not chubby at all. I guess that's why she doesn't mind."

"But how did she get a nickname like that?" Julie wondered.

"It must have something to do with Mardi Gras," Becky mused. "In fact, Mardi Gras actually means Fat Tuesday in French. It's a day when everybody who celebrates Mardi Gras—"

"Like people in Brazil and in New Orleans," Allie interrupted. Allie and Becky were both pretty good students. Leave it to them to know all this.

"Anyway," Becky continued, "everybody pigs out to the max on Fat Tuesday. Get it? For lots of people it's just a fun holiday, but it is traditionally the last day before a season of fasting. That's why they eat so much that day."

"Wow," Julie breathed. "Maybe I should move to Brazil or New Orleans."

Becky reached over and grabbed the pretzel bag out of Julie's hands. "Enough about food," she said sternly. "Will the venerable secretary please continue to read the party notes?"

"Aye, aye, Madam President." Julie pretended to salute. "But you must first explain what Fat Tuesday has to do with Sarah Barrows."

"Beats me." Becky shrugged.

"Simple," Allie said. "Sarah Barrows was born in New Orleans. The Barrows were there for Mardi Gras, and the name just stuck."

"Aha," Julie said. She went back to reading the notes, but I couldn't concentrate on what she was saying. Usually I have a great time at our Party Line meetings, but that day I couldn't keep my mind on business. My throat felt kind of scratchy, and I was only half listening. I was thinking about what Dr. Petrelli, our family doctor, had told me that last time I had had a sore throat.

"One of these days we're going to have to take out those tonsils of yours, Rosie." He had said it as if having my tonsils out wouldn't be a big deal at all. The truth was, though, that I was scared to death.

I once read an article that said it was truly possible to think yourself well. So as I sat there in Becky's attic, I tried to think my throat better. I imagined myself feeling perfectly normal, my throat not aching at all.

My eyes wandered around the attic and happened to light on a giant poster of Vermilion, who is Allie's favorite singer. She had on this fabulous outfit, all spangles and sequins, with sheer, multicolored scarves trailing behind her. That's when the idea hit me. I forgot all about my sore throat and started thinking about the party.

"Hey, I've got it!" I said. "How about a costume skating party?"

"She speaks!" Becky cried, slapping her hand to her forehead. It was true that I'd been pretty quiet during the meeting, but that was because of my throat. It hurt a little to talk, even though I think I *sounded* fine.

"Rosie Torres, you are a genius!" Allie exclaimed.

"Yeah, that's a fantastic idea," Julie agreed. "Do you think it's too late for us to make it into a costume party, though?"

"I don't think so," Becky said, "We did send out the invitations last week, but we can call everyone on the list and let them know. I'm sure they'll love the idea."

"You know . . ." Allie bit her lip while we all looked at her, waiting. "Doesn't everyone dress up in costumes on Mardi Gras and parade around the streets?"

"That's brilliant, Allie!" Julie whooped. "A Mardi Gras ice-skating party!"

"The theme's perfect for Sarah," I exclaimed. I cleared my throat and reached for my glass of soda. I tried to ignore the scratchy feeling I got when I swallowed. *Mind over matter,* I said to myself. *I can think myself well. I am absolutely, positively not getting sick!*

"Do you think Ben Barrow will be at his sister's party?" Julie asked me, wide-eyed. "Not that you'd care, of course," she added innocently.

Julie knew I had a crush on Ben, who is fifteen and, as I've said, the best-looking guy I've ever seen. He works at On Track, the sporting-goods store in the Pine Tree Mall. I've been known on occasion to find a reason to stop into the store when he's working. I need new running shorts. I need a sweatband. I need a new T-shirt. Having a crush on Ben Barrow can get very expensive.

"Well," I said, feigning nonchalance, "he might be there to help out."

Julie snorted. "And I suppose that means you'll be forced to look ravishing. Just in case."

"Well, if anyone can look ravishing, it's Rosie," Allie said.

It's true that I'm pretty good at putting together cool outfits. It helps that my mom has her own boutique, Cinderella, in town. Sometimes I even help her come up with ideas for the front window. I love trying different combinations of colors and textures on the mannequins and seeing what looks interesting.

I love to study fashion magazines, too. I have a subscription to *Saucy*, which I think is the best. Sometimes when I study the fashion pages, I imagine changing things around, adding my own special touches. Then if it feels right, I'll just take a magazine idea and run with it. Nothing is greater than wearing one of my original creations to school and having everyone go crazy over it. (Too bad my mom isn't always as crazy about my experiments as my friends are.)

I also like to experiment on other people. Julie says I see everyone as potential makeover material. Usually my friends are really tolerant about it and let me try all different kinds of makeup, hair, and clothing ideas on them. Sometimes I worry that I'll hurt someone's feelings by suggesting a makeover, but usually the results are great. Of course, once I did blow it completely—on my very best friend! I gave Julie a haircut and I couldn't get the sides exactly even, so somehow her hair kept getting shorter and shorter. At first I thought she was going to kill me, but fortunately she looks terrific in short hair.

One of my most successful makeovers was on Jennifer Peterson, not long after she'd moved to Canfield. I think it did more than just make her look great. I think it also gave her more self-confidence, which helped her make friends. She went from pretty left out and lonely to pretty popular, pretty quickly. Of course, The Party Line helped out, too, with the "Welcome to Canfield" birthday party we gave her right afterward.

Anyway, I had started to plan a really eye-catching costume for the skating party, an outfit that combined Vermilion's flowing scarves with a swirly skirt and lots of bangle bracelets, when suddenly Becky's voice snapped me out of my daydream.

"Can we get back to the subject, which is neither Ben Barrow nor what Rosie could wear to make him fall in love with her?" Becky said. Sometimes it drives her nuts that Julie and I like boys so much.

"Do we want to have a costume theme?" Allie asked.

"Let's say any kind of costume, and let the kids

be creative," Becky said, "but we'll give a prize for best costume."

"We can have an ice-skating parade, sort of like Mardi Gras," Julie said. "And we can bring along Rosie's camera and take pictures of everyone in their costumes. We could give each kid a picture as a party favor. Can we afford the film?" she asked, looking at me. I'm the treasurer, because I'm best in math.

"I think we have enough money. I'll get some film next time I'm at the drugstore," I said. *And maybe I'll get some cough drops while I'm there,* I thought.

"Let's find out what Sarah's costume is going to be, and ask Matthew to decorate her cake like it," Becky suggested. Becky's parents own a restaurant, the Moondance Café, and Matthew makes all the baked goods for the restaurant. He gives us a special professional discount on birthday cakes for our parties.

Finally the meeting ended. Allie was staying to help Becky with her biology homework, so I walked home with Julie. Usually I talk a lot, so it wasn't long before Julie noticed that something was wrong.

"Why do you keep making that noise?" Julie asked me.

"What noise?" I said.

"You keep clearing your throat. You feel okay?"

"Yeah, sure."

Julie looked at me sideways. "You're saying 'yeah, sure,' so why don't I believe 'yeah, sure'?"

I gulped. It hurt. "Well, actually my throat's a little sore," I admitted.

Julie fished a box of cherry-flavored cough drops out of her coat pocket. "Here," she said, handing me the box.

I took one and sucked on it. "Why do you have cough drops?" I asked her.

She shrugged. "I like the taste." I had to laugh, even though it hurt my throat a little. Julie likes anything with sugar in it.

"So, what costume are you going to wear to wow Ben Barrow?" she asked.

Even if it did hurt to talk, I got excited thinking about costume ideas.

"Something exotic," I mused, "something no one else would ever think up, I hope. Something in a color I look great in."

By that time we were standing in front of my house. Julie stared at me. "Well, right now that color would be red, to match your face. Maybe you should take your temperature or something."

"I'm okay," I protested, but I wasn't at all sure that was really true.

"Well, take care of yourself," Julie admonished. "This is going to be a really cool party, and it's going to need that special Rosie touch!"

I had to smile at that. It really helps when your best friend thinks that you make things special.

Two

When I woke up the next morning I felt like someone had dumped gravel down my throat. I still
didn't want to admit I was sick, though. After all,
if I stayed home from school, my parents wouldn't
let me do anything with my friends or work on
Party Line stuff, either. So I got up.

I tried to eat breakfast but it hurt too much to
swallow so I ended up skipping it. Fortunately,
my father was running late and my mother was
getting ready to leave for the boutique to do some
inventory, so neither of them noticed.

Sometimes I walk to school, but that day I took
the bus because it was really cold and I didn't exactly feel up to walking. I sat on the bus in a men-
tal fog until Julie bounced on at her stop.

"Hey, Rosie," she said, falling into the seat next
to me. Then she peered at me more closely and
made a face. "You look horrible," she announced.

"Thanks," I muttered, looking around the bus

for the first time. "Where are Allie and Becky to-day?"

Julie shrugged. "I think they decided to walk. They wanted the time to quiz each other on the Civil War." Mr. Epstein, our history teacher, was giving us a test that day.

"I studied for it a little last night, but I fell asleep early," I said.

Julie sat up and looked at me. "I knew you were sick. You never go to bed early! You *are* sick, aren't you?"

"Give it a rest, Julie. I'm fine."

Julie gave me a haughty look. "Fine. Lie to your best friend."

I felt too awful even to think up a good come-back.

"Here," Julie said, reaching into her coat pocket. "I brought these for you, just in case." In her hand was a box of honey-flavored cough drops. I smiled at her gratefully.

The history test wasn't too bad, and I spent the rest of the morning thinking healthy thoughts. By lunchtime I was congratulating myself on having thought myself well. Just to prove to myself how much better I felt, I got an enormous tuna-fish sandwich and some vanilla pudding from the caf-eteria. By the time I got to our usual table, Allie and Julie were there, and Julie had demolished half a bowl of chili already.

"Hi," she managed between spoonfuls of chili. "You look better!"

I smiled at her. "I feel better. I told you I wasn't sick," I added, biting into the sandwich.

Yeow! When the food hit my throat I thought the pain would knock me onto the floor. Tears actually came to my eyes. Julie swallowed her chili and shook her spoon at me.

"You're not better at all!" she said accusingly.

"I am, really—"

"You are really what?" Becky interrupted, setting down her tray next to mine.

"Sick!" Julie practically screamed. I pushed away my tray, feeling nauseated.

"I'm not sick," I mumbled.

"Do you have a sore throat again?" Allie asked. I nodded. "I remember that one you had last summer. You had to write notes to us instead of talking."

That was true, but I didn't particularly want to be reminded of it just then. Jennifer Peterson happened to be walking by with her lunch tray, and so I waved and called to her to come and join us.

Since our "Welcome to Canfield" party, Jennifer had made a lot of friends, and she would occasionally come sit with the four of us at lunch. It was always a little awkward when she did, though. Not because we didn't all get along or anything; it's just that when four people are as close as Julie, Becky, Allie, and I are, it's hard for someone else to fit right in.

"Hi, Jennifer," I practically croaked. My friends rolled their eyes. "How did you do on the history test?" I asked, sliding over to make room for her.

"Pretty good, I think. Hi, everybody," she said, plunking down her tray.

I couldn't help noticing Jennifer's really cute outfit: a red-and-black polka-dot minidress and black leggings. Her long blond hair was parted on the side, and she had woven a few strands of hair into a narrow braid. Since the makeover I'd done on her, she was always trying great new hairstyles.

"Great dress," I said. "Where'd you get it?"

"Winter's. I spent all my birthday money on it!" she said with a laugh. I nodded. A really great outfit is always worth blowing your budget.

My friends had been unusually quiet ever since Jennifer sat down at the table. It wasn't that they didn't like Jennifer; it was that old insider-outsider thing. Jennifer still seemed like an outsider, especially with all four of us.

"So, um, how's Bear?" I asked. Bear is Jennifer's gigantic dog.

"He's sick!" she said, looking worried. "He

wouldn't eat at all yesterday." That sounded serious. Bear usually eats everything in sight. "We're taking him to the vet right after school," Jennifer told us.

"Oh, poor Bear," said Becky. She loves animals, and is even thinking about becoming a veterinarian.

"My parents think he might have caught a virus from my cousins' kitten."

"Can dogs catch things from cats?" Allie asked.

Jennifer shrugged. "The vet said it's possible. My cousins visited us last week and they brought their kitten, Alfie. Anyway, Alfie seemed like he had a cold or something. But Bear saw Alfie and fell in love! He followed Alfie around all day and kept nuzzling him."

"I wish I had a picture of that!" Julie laughed. Anything that has to do with cats really gets Julie. "It must have been so cute, that huge, shaggy dog trying to mother a tiny, fluffy, kitten."

Jennifer laughed, too. "It really was. When Alfie sneezed, Bear's eyes got all big. He was so worried about his baby!"

All my friends laughed, but I couldn't do much more than smile, my throat hurt so much. I couldn't even eat my pudding. Of course, Julie being Julie, she noticed right away.

"You're not eating," she accused as she polished off her second dessert.

"I'm not very hungry," I lied. I shoved my mostly uneaten lunch across the table. "Here, you eat it."

Julie pushed it back and sighed. "Thanks but no thanks. You're sick, whether you admit it or not, and I don't want to catch it."

I hadn't thought of that. Allie put her hand on my forehead. "I think you have a fever, Rosie."

"Could we just change the subject?" I asked.

I was literally saved by the bell. We gathered up our books and headed out of the lunchroom.

After Jennifer had gone off toward her locker, Allie said, "So we're going to the mall after school for the party supplies, right?"

"Right," said Becky.

"Let's meet at the side door right after school," Allie said.

"Sounds good to me," Julie said. I turned around to head for my next class, but Julie stopped me.

"Rosie?"

I raised my eyebrows so I wouldn't have to talk.

"Take it easy this afternoon, okay?"

I gave her a thumbs-up sign, as if everything were just fine. Julie just shook her head and went into the classroom. Sometimes it's a pain when your best friend knows you so well.

Three

"Don't look now, but there's Ben Barrow!" Julie hissed.

We had just entered the mall and were heading toward The Perfect Party to get our supplies. Ben was walking toward us, sipping a can of soda. Usually I would make the most of any opportunity to run into Ben, but I was feeling so rotten I didn't want to talk to anyone. Not even Ben! I dawdled behind Julie, trying to hide, but Ben saw us and walked right over.

"Hi, how's it going?" he asked. I noticed that he looked even cuter than usual, in a blue cotton shirt that exactly matched the color of his dreamy eyes.

"Great," said Julie, grinning at him. She nudged me and I edged out from behind her.

"Yeah, great," I said softly.

"So, you guys are giving my little sister's birthday party, right?" Ben asked us.

"Right," said Becky. "We're giving her an ice-skating party at Van Fleet Park."

"Sounds great," Ben said. "Sarah really loves to skate. My parents gave her ice skates for her birthday last year and she's practically worn them out already."

As rotten as I felt, I really wanted to know if Ben was going to be at his little sister's party. I figured I couldn't come right out and ask him, but fortunately Julie had no such qualms.

"Will you and Liz be at the party?" she asked. "We just want to get an idea of how many older kids will be there," she added innocently.

"The party's Sa-Saturday," Allie added shyly. Sometimes when Allie is nervous she stammers a little. I smiled at her. Ever since she started liking Dylan Matthews she's been a lot more courageous about talking to guys.

"Yeah, I'll be there," said Ben easily. "Well, I've got to go to work. Catch you later," he said, walking off toward On Track.

I watched him head down the mall. "Tell me he isn't the cutest guy you've ever seen," I murmured dreamily (and, to tell the truth, a little hoarsely).

"Someone get me the barf bag," said Becky.

"That's about the quietest I've ever seen you be

around him," Allie commented as we looked in the windows of Winter's department store.

"Yeah," Julie agreed. "If that's not proof that she's sick, nothing is."

"I like that lime green shirt and skirt," I said, pointing to an outfit in the window.

"It's not a good color on blonds," said Julie, shaking her own short blond hair, "but with your dark coloring, you'd look great in it. Want to go try it on?"

"I don't have any money," I said, stalling.

"Since when has that ever stopped you from trying on clothes?" she asked with a laugh.

Julie was right. I'll try on clothes with ten cents in my pocket. That's one of the reasons I love The Party Line. Not only do I get to have a blast with my best friends, but I make enough money to occasionally afford one of the outfits I try on. (It also helps that my mom owns a boutique. I have been known to beg my way into an outfit or two from her store.)

"I just don't feel like trying on clothes today," I told Julie.

"Quick!" yelled Julie. "Call the paramedics! Call nine-one-one! Rosie doesn't feel like trying on clothes!"

"Come on," said Becky exasperatedly, "we'd

better get going. We have a lot of party shopping to do, remember?"

The Perfect Party is a great store. They have a huge selection of terrific, unusual decorations, supplies, and prizes that we use to create fantastic parties. We took one of the hot-pink plastic hand-baskets and started down the aisle.

"What do you think of these?" Becky asked, holding up some blue paper plates with white snowflakes on them. "Good for a winter skating party, don't you think?"

"Kind of boring," Julie said, making a face.

"Hey, look at this!" Allie cried, pointing to a new display. It had a huge cardboard cut-out of a court jester standing with a mysterious-looking gypsy. A banner stretched between the two figures had the words *Mardi Gras* printed in silver letters.

"I'm impressed," said Julie. "They heard about our party plans and ordered a special shipment just for us."

"Look at these!" Becky said, picking up a package of Mardi Gras paper napkins. "They're perfect. They've got all this authentic Mardi Gras stuff right here!"

"Are we serving theme food at the party?" Julie wondered. (Leave it to Julie to bring up the food angle.)

"What about a Mardi Gras dessert?" Becky asked.

"You *would* want to know about dessert," I said.

"I know!" Allie suddenly shrieked. "We can have king cake!"

"I know what that is!" I said, surprised. I don't know why I hadn't thought of it sooner. King cake is like a coffee cake, but wonderfully sweet and really moist and fabulously rich. One of my parents' friends sent us one during Mardi Gras last year. It came by mail order all the way from New Orleans. King cake is decorated in the traditional Mardi Gras colors of gold, green and purple, and the best thing about it is the king baby doll hidden inside the cake. Excitedly I told my friends about it, but I accidentally overdid it and my throat began to hurt. I took a quiet break and let Allie and Becky finish telling Julie for me.

"King baby doll?" Julie was saying when I stopped thinking about my sore throat long enough to focus on the conversation once again.

"Well, it's really just a doll," Becky explained. "In the old days they were sometimes made of china but now they're mostly made of plastic."

"But why?" Julie wondered. "What's the point?"

"Well," Allie picked up the story, "in New Orleans they have king cakes from Twelfth Night—

that's the twelfth night after Christmas—right up until Mardi Gras. Anyway, after they have the first Twelfth Night party, the person who gets the doll gives the party the next week, and so on up until Mardi Gras."

"School kids do it, too," Becky said. "One child brings in a king cake the week of Twelfth Night, and then whoever gets the doll brings the cake in the next week and so on."

"What a great custom!" Julie raved.

"The person who gets the doll is also king for the day," Becky said, "and gets to wear a cardboard crown. Sometimes they even get to tell everyone else what to do."

"Kids will really love the idea of a hidden surprise in the cake," Allie said.

"Can we get a king cake?" Julie asked.

"Well, it's pretty much like a coffee cake with different colored icing," Becky said. "Why don't I ask Matthew if he can whip one up for us?"

"Good idea," Julie agreed. "Ask him what sort of surprise will bake well, and we'll get one to hide in the cake. Then whoever gets it will win a special prize."

"Like what?" practical Allie asked.

"Mmmm," Julie said, picking up an adorable necklace from the display. A ceramic pendant in the shape of a clown's face was strung on a long, silky black cord. The clown's eyes were tiny green jewels. "This is only five-ninety-five and it would make a great prize for the person who finds the doll in the cake," Julie said.

"At Mardi Gras they give out plastic beads and colored coins to everyone, too," Allie added, pointing to a selection of beads and coins under the Mardi Gras display. "These would make great favors, and they'd really make the party authentic."

Allie pulled out her information sheet and checked our budget for the four-hundredth time. "We can do it," she said. It went into the basket, along with Mardi Gras colored streamers and paper plates and cups in the same colors.

"I have an idea that won't cost money," Becky said. "What if we went to a travel agent and asked if they had any Mardi Gras posters they could spare. Then we can tack them up on the posts around the skating rink or on the trees to create a little atmosphere."

"Great idea!" Allie was always enthusiastic about anything we could get for free. She worried a lot about our bottom line, especially since she had made a mistake on our very first job estimate and we'd almost ended up working for free.

"Can anyone go to the travel agent with me after school tomorrow?" Becky wanted to know.

"Let's go right now," I said. "There's a travel agency at the other end of the mall."

We started walking. "What's your costume going to be, Julie?" I asked.

Julie shrugged. "I don't know. I haven't come up with a good idea yet."

Becky made a face. "I hate this part of it. I mean, it's cute for the kids but I can't stand dressing up in some stupid outfit."

"Oh, come on, Becky, it'll be fun," I said, nudging her elbow.

"Fun for you, maybe. I'm just not good at costumes."

"Hey, I've got an idea," I said.

"Yeah?" Becky looked glum.

"What about Miss Laura? Who would know more about costumes than she does?"

Miss Laura is Becky's adopted grandmother. She lives at Pine Villa, the same retirement complex where Allie's grandmother lives. Miss Laura used to be a professional singer and dancer in the Chicago Follies. She has trunks and trunks full of costumes and makeup from her show-business days, and she helped us when we were working on Becky's costume and makeup for the school play.

"Yeah, I bet she'd love to help us," said Allie.

Becky's face looked like the sun had come out

after a thunderstorm. "I'll call her," she said, "and see if we can all go over there tomorrow."

"I've been wanting to see the inside of those trunks ever since she helped us with your Juliet costume. Now I'll finally get my chance!" I said to Becky.

As excited as I was about our Mardi Gras party, I was really feeling rotten. When no one was looking I put my hand up to my forehead. I could tell I had a fever. There was no getting around it: I was sick.

"Listen, you guys," I said, stopping. "I'm not feeling so hot."

"At least you finally admitted it," said Julie. "Do you want to go home?"

"No." I sighed. "But I guess I should."

"We'll walk you home," Allie said loyally.

"No way!" I answered quickly. "I mean it! We've got a lot of work to do for this party. I can get myself home."

"Are you sure?" asked Julie doubtfully.

"Sure I'm sure," I answered.

Becky looked at Julie. "Is she being nice or does she mean it?" Becky asked.

Julie looked at me thoughtfully. "She means it," she decided. "But," she added to me, "call me right after dinner and tell me how you are. Promise?"

"Promise," I answered. I waved good-bye and

headed in the other direction. After I'd taken a few steps, though, I turned and looked at my friends. They were laughing, and it looked like they were having a great time. I sighed and walked through the automatic sliding doors. I dreaded going home and telling my parents that I felt sick. I could hear Dr. Petrelli's words echoing in my mind: "One of these days we're going to have to take out those tonsils of yours, Rosie." I was really afraid that this was "one of these days!"

Four

Sure enough, as soon as I got home my mother called Dr. Petrelli's office. He wanted to see me the very next day.

I have this rule of thumb: the worse you feel, the better you should dress. So the next morning I picked out the outfit I was going to wear to the doctor's office with great care. I put on my black denim miniskirt and a lavender silk T-shirt (a Cinderella special!) and tossed a purple-and-gold paisley vest over it. I wore lavender tights and flat black lace-up ankle boots. Then I threw my head back and brushed my hair from underneath, which gives it more body. I put on a touch of mauve eyeshadow and just a hint of blush and lip gloss. Whatever horrors were going to happen, I was going to look good for them.

The only good thing I can say about doctors' offices is that they don't smell as bad as dentists' offices. I sat down on the couch in the waiting room while my mother told the nurse we'd arrived. I know everyone who works there pretty well, since I've been going there for years. I especially like Dr. Petrelli's nurse, Tori Sweeney. She's really pretty and manages to look great even in a nurse's uniform. She's only about twenty-five or so and she always tells me to call her Tori instead of Ms. Sweeney. Tori waved at me from the office and I gave her a half-hearted wave back.

My mom came back and sat down next to me. "Look, Rosie, here's the latest issue of *Saucy*," she said, handing me the magazine from the table.

I just shrugged. I knew she was trying to cheer me up and take my mind off my throat, but I couldn't help myself.

"Oh, Rosie," Mom said, stroking my forehead, "I wish I could magically take away the pain, but I can't."

"Do you think I'll have to have my tonsils out?" I asked.

"I don't know. Maybe."

I sighed.

"Listen, it won't be so bad—" my mom started to say, but just then Tori came into the waiting room and called my name.

"Rosie, Dr. Petrelli will see you now. Come right this way." She smiled her usual friendly smile. I tried to smile back, but all I could think was that it was easy to smile when you only worked at the doctor's office and were otherwise perfectly healthy.

"Should I come, too?" asked my mom, getting up from her seat.

"Whatever Rosie prefers is fine," said Tori. That was the first time she had asked me; before it had just always been assumed that my mom would come in with me. I decided to go in alone, even though a part of me really wanted my mother right there next to me.

"I'll go by myself," I said. My mom smiled encouragingly.

"Dr. Petrelli will talk to you in his office afterward," Tori told her.

I walked into the examining room and hoisted myself onto the examination table. The white paper covering the table crinkled under me as I sat down. Tori put a thermometer under my tongue and took my blood pressure. Then she did the thing I really hate: she took a blood test. Tori knows how I feel about it, though. She lets me know when she's about to stick the needle in my arm, and I look the other way. Simple, really—but I still hate it.

Finally Tori patted my shoulder and told me the doctor would be right in, and then she left. I swung my legs back and forth and tried to hum a Vermilion song, "It Takes Rain to Make a Rainbow," under my breath. I thought it would help me to be less nervous, but it just made my throat hurt.

After what seemed like forever Dr. Petrelli came into the examining room with a jovial look on his face. Easy for him.

"Hi, Rosie," he said as he looked over my chart. He felt the glands in my neck, and I winced a little. "Hurts, huh?" he said sympathetically. I nodded miserably. There didn't seem to be any point in lying to the doctor.

"How's your business enterprise going?" he asked me as he got out the instrument he uses to look down people's throats. I had told him about The Party Line the last time I'd come in with one of my sore throats. I was very flattered that he remembered.

"It's going great." I managed to say.

"My wife and I will have to remember to give you a call for our daughter Amy's birthday party. Open wide." Dr. Petrelli stuck a tongue depressor in my mouth and looked down my throat while shining a bright light on me. "You've got a lot of inflammation in there," he said.

The doctor straightened up and threw away the tongue depressor. "Well, Rosie," he said, "I think it's time we got rid of those tonsils."

My heart sank. Those were the words I least wanted to hear!

"Couldn't I just take penicillin?" I asked. "That's what you gave me last time, and the sore throat went away."

He smiled at me kindly. "Believe me, Rosie, I know how you feel. I've been hoping we could avoid surgery in your case, but I don't see any way around it this time. I know it's a pain in the neck," he said, and we both groaned at the pun, "but if we take care of the problem right now, you won't have to go through this again."

I nodded. I knew he was right, but I wished it weren't true.

Tori knocked on the door and came in. "I think we're finished here," Dr. Petrelli told her. "I'm going to call the hospital, and then I'd like to see Rosie and Mrs. Torres in my office."

Tori gave me a small sympathetic smile and left to get my mother.

For a minute or two I just sat on the edge of the table, feeling numb. And scared. Then I hopped down and headed for Dr. Petrelli's private office. I was just settling into a big comfy armchair across from my mother when he walked in.

Dr. Petrelli sat down behind his desk. "This time I really feel her tonsils have to come out," he told my mother. "We don't routinely take out tonsils anymore. They seem to act as a barrier to certain infections, so we like to try to treat patients with antibiotics and keep the tonsils intact," he explained. "But in Rosie's case I'd say we have too strong a history of repeated infections. There's a bed available at the hospital, and I'd like to admit her right away. We can do the surgery tomorrow morning."

Boy! Talk about not wasting time!

"All right, Dr. Petrelli," Mom said.

"Will you take them out yourself?" I asked. My voice sounded normal, but I was surprised it wasn't quavering. I was so nervous!

"Absolutely," he assured me.

Dr. Petrelli must have seen how scared I looked. "I promise you, Rosie, you won't feel a thing. You'll be asleep when I take them out, and it will be over before you know it. You'll have a bit of a sore throat afterward, but you'll get to eat lots of ice cream, so it's not so bad."

"How long will I have to stay in the hospital?" I asked.

"Only two or three days," he said.

"But I have to be better by Saturday. We're giving an important party on Saturday," I explained. I couldn't miss Sarah Barrow's skating party. I just couldn't!

"I'm really sorry, Rosie, but you won't be all better by Saturday," Dr. Petrelli said.

I stared down at the floor. This was just terrible!

"I'd suggest that you go home, pack a small bag, and go on over to Canfield General," he said kindly. "I'll be over to see you this evening. I'll explain everything then and answer any questions you have about the operation. I'm sorry this is ruining your party plans," he added.

Dr. Petrelli is a nice doctor, but his being sorry didn't help me any. I felt absolutely miserable as we drove home. I was going to miss what would probably be our best party of the year. Not only that, but Ben Barrow would be there, and I wouldn't!

Five

My mom came up to my room with me to help me pack for the hospital. Just as we were finishing, the doorbell rang.

"I'll get it. Why don't you pick out some books or magazines to take with you?" my mom suggested on her way out.

I half-heartedly packed the last two issues of *Saucy*, even though I'd already read them. I decided to pack my Walkman, along with some Bastille cassettes. I also tossed in a sketch pad and my colored pencils, though I didn't think I'd feel much like drawing.

Just as I was stuffing all this into my overnight bag, I heard voices downstairs. The next thing I knew, Julie, Allie, and Becky were crowding into my bedroom.

"We came to see how you're feeling," Julie said.

I was really glad that my friends were there.

"Rotten," I admitted, sitting down on my bed, "but I'm glad you guys came over."

"So what did the doctor say?" Becky asked. She settled down on my rose-colored carpet. Julie and Allie sat on the pillows underneath my cabinets.

I sighed. "He says I have to have my tonsils out. Tomorrow!"

"Tomorrow?" Julie echoed. "Wow, he doesn't waste any time."

I nodded grimly.

"I'm packing," I said, pointing to my overnight bag. "We're leaving for the hospital as soon as I'm done."

Allie's eyes got wide. *"Now?"*

"As in this minute?" Julie asked.

"Yeah," I answered. "Can you believe it?"

"Well, it gives you less time to be scared," Becky said. "Not that you should be scared or anything," she added hastily.

I ran my finger over the flowered pattern of my bedspread. "The worst part is that I won't be better by Saturday. The doctor says I can't go to Sarah's party."

"That's horrible!" said Julie. "Maybe you'll heal more quickly than he thinks?" she asked optimistically.

I shook my head. "He didn't sound too hopeful."

"That's rotten luck," Allie said sympathetically.

"Tell me about it," I said. "I know this party is going to be a lot of work. Plus I was really looking forward to it. I'm sorry, you guys."

"It's not your fault!" Julie said. "We'll just each have to do a little extra, that's all. We've managed it before."

"Remember when I had the talent contest?" Allie reminded me.

"And when Julie broke her leg?" Becky added.

I sighed. "I just can't believe I have to miss this party."

"We'll save you some king cake," Allie offered. "And we'll take lots of pictures to show you afterward. Uh, can we borrow your camera?" It's always been my job to take pictures. I handed Allie my camera.

"Thanks, Allie. Could you take about a hundred shots of Ben Barrow?"

"I think he'd notice if we used up all the film on him," Julie said with a laugh. "But I promise we'll get at least one good one of him for you."

"You'll have to freeze the king cake. I don't think I'll be eating much besides Jell-O and ice cream for a while," I said.

My mom stuck her head into my room. "All packed?"

"Yep," I said.

"Good. You girls can talk a little longer. I'm going to call your father at the office," she said, and disappeared.

"Boy, I'm really going to miss your help with our costumes," Becky said. "Miss Laura may come up with something great, but who'll help me get it right when I wear it the day of the party?"

"Too bad Jennifer Peterson isn't coming," I mused. "The Juliet costume she made you was great." Just as I said that, I got an idea. "Hey, wait a minute. You need extra help and Jennifer is really good with costumes. How about if you ask her to help with the party?"

Julie looked at me as if I was crazy. "No way. She's not part of The Party Line." Allie and Becky nodded, backing Julie up.

I have to admit that secretly I felt a little happy that my friends didn't want to replace me, but I really did want them to have some help. "I know she isn't part of The Party Line," I said, "but I bet she'd be happy to help you out just this once."

"I don't like it," said Julie firmly.

"Maybe it's not such a bad idea," said Becky tentatively. "I mean, we really could use the help. Jennifer's pretty nice."

"Yeah? You used to hate her guts," Julie reminded her.

"Well, I got to know her better. We all did," Becky pointed out.

"I don't care—" Julie started to say as my mom popped back into my room.

"Okay, I spoke with your dad," she said. "He's going to meet us at the hospital. We should be going soon," she told me.

"Sure, Mom," I said. "I'll be down in five minutes."

I turned to my friends. "Look, promise me you'll at least think about it, okay?"

Allie and Becky nodded slowly. Julie scowled. "Please?" I coaxed her. "If you won't do it for me, would you at least do it for The Party Line?"

"All right, all right," Julie said with a scowl. "I'll *think* about it."

"Good," I said with relief. I knew I'd feel a lot less anxious about Sarah's party if my friends had some help.

I zipped up my overnight bag.

"Well, I guess I have to go."

"We'll miss you," said Julie.

The four of us walked downstairs. My mom was waiting with the car keys in her hand.

"Will we be allowed to visit Rosie?" Julie asked my mom.

"I'll find out," my mother promised. "You ready, Rosie?"

I sighed. "As ready as I'll ever be."

We all walked out into the late-afternoon sunshine. "It'll be over before you know it," Becky said encouragingly.

"I'll get all your homework assignments for you," Allie volunteered.

My friends crowded around the car as I got in.

"Bye! Bye!" they called to me.

My mom started the car and I rolled down the window and waved back to them. I turned around in the seat and watched as the three of them grew smaller and smaller in the distance. I turned back around in my seat.

"You're lucky to have such good friends," my mom said.

"Yeah, they're great," I agreed. I was quiet for a minute. "Mom, is it going to hurt? Tell me the truth."

"I wouldn't lie to you, Rosie," my mom said. "The truth is, I really don't know. I think you should ask Dr. Petrelli all your questions when you see him tonight. I'll tell you what: we'll write them all down when we get into your room so that we don't forget any of them. How's that?"

"Okay," I agreed. Then I added, "Hey, Mom, are you allowed to wear makeup when you have surgery?"

My mom laughed all the way to the hospital.

Six

When I first checked into my room at Canfield
General Hospital I was all alone. The other bed
was empty. My dad arrived right after we did with
a pint of my favorite ice cream, Cherry Garcia. All
the not-eating I'd been doing had taken its toll: I
finished the whole pint by myself!

I tried not to think too much about the surgery,
or about how disappointed I was that I wouldn't
be able to go to Sarah's party on Saturday. I suppose I was feeling a little sorry for myself. At least
I was able to wear my favorite rose-colored quilted
satin bathrobe with the white lace collar instead
of the hideous cotton wrap thing that the hospital
provided.

Just as I was starting on my second game of
Chinese checkers with my dad, the door to my
room swung open. There stood a short, thin girl,
about my age, with tons of frizzy black curls, pale
skin, and the biggest hazel eyes I'd ever seen. She

carried a gym bag over her shoulder and acted as if she belonged in my room. Which, as it turned out, she did.

"Hi, I'm Skye Friedman, your roommate. Hey, they gave me one of the good rooms this time," she added, looking around approvingly. "Usually I get a view of the parking lot." Our room looked out onto a woody park.

"I'm Rosie Torres," I said.

"And these must be your parental units," Skye said, grinning at my parents. "Mine are downstairs, still doing the Paperwork Shuffle."

My parents looked sort of bewildered, but they smiled nicely and told Skye it was nice to meet her.

A teenage girl wearing a pink uniform stuck her head into the room. "Skye! Bonnie told me you were here. You look great!"

"Hi, Angela. Yeah, I'm feeling terrif. Poker later?"

Angela winked. "Are you kidding? I had to empty out my piggy bank the last time you were here."

Skye grinned. "Yeah, I'm a demon at five-card stud. Catch you later!" she called to Angela, who waved and disappeared down the hall.

"You've, um, been here before?" I asked tentatively.

"Lots," Skye confirmed.

I really wanted to know what could be wrong with Skye that she'd spend so much time in the hospital, but it seemed rude to ask. Besides, except for being very pale, she looked perfectly healthy to me.

Skye put some of her stuff away and then went down to the nurses' station to visit some friends. She really must be here a lot, I thought. My mom got out a pad of paper for me to write down all my questions for Dr. Petrelli. We finished the list just as he arrived.

"Well, I see you're all settled in, Rosie," he said. "That's a very pretty robe."

"Thanks," I said.

"We'll be taking your tonsils out about nine o'clock tomorrow morning. Is there anything that you want to know about the procedure?"

I went through my list and asked Dr. Petrelli my questions. He was really nice and patient and answered every one of them. He even complimented me for asking them.

"I'd like to see more people taking charge and learning about their own health care," Dr. Petrelli said, which really made me feel good.

The last question on my list had to do with the party on Saturday. I figured I might as well try one last shot. "Dr. Petrelli, if I heal really fast is there any chance I can go to the party on Saturday?"

The doctor looked at me with regret. "I can tell it means a lot to you, Rosie, but it's really not a good idea. It will most likely be your first full day home from the hospital and you'll need your rest."

I sighed and finally accepted the inevitable. I really was going to miss the Mardi Gras ice-skating party.

My parents left shortly after Dr. Petrelli did, promising me they'd be back to see me as soon as I woke up after the operation. I started leafing through a copy of *Saucy* magazine. Then Skye bopped back into the room.

"Don't look now," she said, "but they're coming around with the bow-wow buffet."

"The what?" I asked her.

"I think of it as dog-food dining. You know—dinner." Skye explained.

"The food is no good, huh?" I said.

"To put it mildly," she said, holding her nose.

Angela, the nurse's aide in the pink uniform, wheeled in a cart of food.

Skye just shook her head. "Angela, Angela, you know I don't eat that junk."

Angela grinned at Skye. "I suppose it was silly of me, thinking you might have turned over a new leaf." She brought a covered dish over to me.

"Getting your tonsils out, huh? That's why they gave you all soft stuff," Angela explained, "so it won't hurt your sore throat."

I lifted the metal cover and stared down at two soft-boiled eggs and a dish of creamed spinach. Next to it was a mound of lime Jell-O. Yuck!

"As you can see, I didn't lie," Skye said.

"I'm not very hungry, anyway," I said.

Angela shrugged. "Well, you should try to eat something. I'll leave it here in case you change your mind." She turned to Skye. "I suppose there's no point in leaving yours?"

"Fat chance," said Skye. Angela just shook her head and wheeled the food cart down the hall.

Skye picked up the phone by her bed and dialed a number. "Hello," she said, "is Jessica Cantor in?" Skye turned to me while she waited. "I got you covered, roomie. What appeals to your palate?"

"My what?" I asked in confusion.

Just then Skye spoke into the phone. "Hi, Aunt Jessica, it's me," she said. "Right . . . right . . . Just the usual. Oh, and could you add, say, two orders of chocolate mousse? Just a sec." Skye covered the mouthpiece and looked at me. "You like chocolate?" she asked me.

"Sure," I said, totally bewildered.

"Yeah, that'll be fine, said Skye into the phone."

"Great! Bye, Aunt Jessica." She hung up the phone. "Dinner will be here in about a half-hour."

"From where?" I asked her.

"Jessica's Pantry on High Street. That's my Aunt Jessica's business."

"That was where my parents got the food for their anniversary party last year," I remembered. "It was great."

"Yeah, Aunt Jessica's a whiz in the kitchen. Want to watch TV?" Skye asked me.

"Sure," I said. Skye grabbed the remote control and tuned in to a baseball game, which she watched avidly. I snuck peeks at her out of the corner of my eye. Why would someone who seemed healthy spend a lot of time in the hospital?

"Where do you go to school?" I asked Skye.

"Midvale Middle School. I'm in seventh grade. How about you?" Skye asked me.

Midvale is the next town over from us. I know a few kids at Midvale Middle School from track meets, because I'm on Canfield Middle School's track team.

"I'm in seventh at Canfield. Hey, do you know Karen Anderson? She's on the track team."

"No, I'm not real athletic. I follow baseball, though," Skye said.

We talked about sports for a while. Soon a pretty

young woman came into the room carrying a picnic hamper.

"Aunt Jessica!" Skye exclaimed. "You've rescued me! Let's see what you brought! This is my roommate, Rosie Torres," she added.

"Hi Rosie. I'm Jessica Cantor, Cecilia's aunt."

"Cecilia?" I asked, thoroughly confused.

Skye waved her hand through the air. "They named me Cecilia. Do I look like a Cecilia? I changed it to Skye." She dove into the picnic hamper. "Pâté! French bread! Raspberry tarts!"

Skye pulled out a tart and bit into it. "Heavenly." She sighed.

Her aunt shook her head, "Must you always eat dessert first?"

Skye shrugged. "It all ends up in the same place, so why worry about the order?"

Skye's aunt pulled a container out of the hamper and handed it to me. "This is for you. A double order of my Death by Chocolate."

"This is unbelievable," I marveled as the cool, chocolatey dessert slid down my throat. "Thanks, Ms. Cantor."

"Call me Jessica," she said, smiling warmly. I ate some more of the mousse. So far, being in the hospital wasn't bad at all!

Jessica stayed and watched a couple of innings of the Red Sox game with Skye, then she left.

That's when Skye finally changed into her pajamas—a long T-shirt that read I've Seen Elvis. It had lots of cartoons of Elvis Presley in different disguises printed on the front. It was hilarious.

"Very soon we get to the best part," Skye said mysteriously, plopping back down on her bed.

"Best part of what?" I asked her.

"Who do you think is the cutest guy in the world?" she asked me.

The name Ben Barrow popped into my mind. But I didn't want to think about Ben, which would only remind me of the party I wasn't going to. "Hmm . . . I'd say Dave Mathey," I decided. He's the lead singer for Bastille and is absolutely gorgeous.

"Wrong," said Skye, her eyes dancing. "He's second cutest. Dr. Jeff is the cutest."

Just as I was about to ask who Dr. Jeff was, the door opened. There stood a young doctor handsome enough to be a rock star any day of the week. He had wavy blond hair and a great tan. All I could do was stare at him.

"Told you so," Skye said, grinning at me.

"I guess you just couldn't stay away from me, huh, Skye?" asked Dr. Jeff, walking over to her bed. "How are you feeling?"

"Great. No problems," said Skye breezily.

Dr. Jeff turned to me. "Hi, I'm Dr. Behrman,

but special patients like Skye and you can call me Dr. Jeff." He turned his thousand-watt smile on me, and I had to smile back. Dr. Jeff was cuter than the actors who played doctors on soap operas. And just think—besides being gorgeous, he could even save lives. It seemed incredibly romantic to me, being a doctor. *Maybe I should consider a career in medicine,* I thought. *Doctor Torres, sports-medicine practitioner to the stars!*

"Excuse us for a minute," Dr. Jeff said to me. I blinked and came back to reality.

"Oh, sure," I said, and smiled at him. He smiled back and then drew the curtain around Skye's bed. He talked to her in a quiet tone of voice and I couldn't hear a thing. After a little while he drew back the curtain.

"Okay, girls, try not to create a riot on the floor tonight. I'll be in to see you in the morning, Skye," he said as he walked out the door.

"Tell me he isn't even cuter than Dave Mathey," Skye challenged me.

"He's unbelievably cute," I agreed. "But doesn't that make you feel funny, having him examine you and everything?"

"Well . . ." Skye was quiet for a moment. I was worried that I'd upset her, but then she perked up. "If I felt funny about that I'd *really* be sick!" she cackled.

The phone by my bed rang.

"Hello?"

"Hi, this is Ben Barrow," said a voice I recognized as Julie's.

"Funny, Ben," I said, playing along, "I never realized your voice was so high." Then I added, "This is so great, Julie. How did you get my phone number?"

"From your mom, silly," said Julie. "We're calling from Miss Laura's. We wanted to make sure you were okay."

"Yeah, I'm fine. I had Death by Chocolate for dinner!"

"You had what?" Julie asked.

"Never mind. I'll explain some other time."

"Miss Laura is helping us with our costumes. She's got some really great ideas," Julie said.

"You saw her costume trunks?" I said, absolutely green with envy.

"Yeah, but she says to tell you—oh, hold on, she wants to tell you herself."

Miss Laura got on the phone. "Rosie, dear," she boomed in her husky voice.

"Hi, Miss Laura," I said.

"I want you to know, my dear, that I consider us kindred spirits. Someone with your creative flair really must not be denied a chance at my costume trunks. You and I will definitely go through them together when you're better."

"Thanks, Miss Laura. I just hate to miss seeing them now—"

"Enough of that," Miss Laura interrupted. "We'll have scads of time to do it."

"I know, but I really wanted to be at the party on Saturday."

"Ah, the party. My advice to you is to look at the big picture."

"The big picture?" I asked, not having a clue what she meant.

"Well, it's my understanding that you like a certain young man who will be at this party. Is that so?"

"Yes," I said with a grin.

"If you aren't at the party, he'll wonder where you are and be that much more intrigued with you, my dear," Miss Laura explained patiently.

"But Miss Laura, I don't even know if he knows I'm alive—romantically speaking, that is."

"Any boy that could fail to notice how totally unique and special you are is, by definition, not worth your attention. You remember that," she instructed me.

"I will," I answered. She had a point there.

"Your friends want to talk to you again," said Miss Laura. "See you soon, dear!"

"Hi, Rosie. Are you okay?" asked Becky.

"Not bad," I said. "Kind of nervous, though."

"Yeah, I would be, too. But I'm sure you'll be fine. Allie wants to say hello," she said.

"Hi, Rosie. Listen, I know being in the hospital isn't the greatest, but don't forget you'll get to eat tons of ice cream after the tonsillectomy."

I smiled. "Thanks for the encouragement," I said.

"Gee, you don't even sound depressed," Allie marveled.

"Well, so far being in the hospital has been kind of entertaining," I said. "Listen, Allie, are you guys okay for Sarah's party Saturday?" I asked.

"We voted on whether or not to call Jennifer," Allie said.

"And?" I asked her.

"Well, it was two to one for calling her. But we decided it had to be unanimous."

"Put Julie on," I told Allie.

"Yeah?" came Julie's voice.

"Listen, I know you voted against calling Jennifer, and I just want to say that I think you should change your vote."

"Hey, it was supposed to be a secret ballot!" Julie protested.

"I know you too well," I said. "Seriously, you should call her."

"All right," Julie grumbled. "But it just won't be the same."

"Of course it won't be the same," I said. "It's not *supposed* to be the same. It's just supposed to help!"

My throat was really starting to hurt from talking so much. "Listen, I have to go. Say good-bye to Allie and Becky and Miss Laura for me, okay? Hey, can you guys call me tomorrow afternoon?" I added. "You know, after I, uh, have them out?" I didn't want to actually say the word *surgery*.

"You bet," said Julie. "Bye."

I hung up the phone, glad that they were going to call Jennifer for some help. I glanced over at Skye, who had closed her eyes. She looked a little pale. As I was staring at her she opened her eyes and looked at me. "Guess I'm a little tired after all," she murmured.

"Me, too," I agreed quickly.

"You nervous about getting your tonsils out?" she asked me.

"A little," I admitted. "It seems creepy, having surgery while you're asleep and can't feel anything."

Skye shrugged. "Don't worry. It sounds weirder than it really is. I've had lots of operations."

"You have?" I asked her. "On what?"

"My heart. I was born with a hole in my heart,

and that messes up my lungs. They've been trying to fix it for years," she said matter-of-factly.

"That sounds scary," I said in a little voice.

She shrugged again. "I'm used to it, I guess. The crummy part is that they won't let me do a lot of things, like play baseball, for example. And I get out of breath easily. Like if I run. Anyway, Dr. Jeff thinks the technique they're going to use this time might be able to repair it completely, and then I won't have to have any more surgery."

"That would be great."

"Yeah," she agreed. Skye snuggled down underneath the covers, yawning. "Anyway, roomie, you'll be fine tomorrow. Don't worry." She closed her eyes.

I looked over at her. I wondered what it felt like to have a hole in your heart, or not to be able to run. Suddenly having my tonsils out didn't seem like such a big thing after all.

Seven

I woke up on Wednesday morning with Skye's face peering down at me. "Did you know your nostrils twitch when you're sleeping?" she asked me.

Maybe I'm having some weird dream, I thought. I started to sit up, but I felt a little dizzy.

"How are you feeling, honey?" It was my mom, leaning over my bed.

I opened my mouth to ask her if it was over, but I could hardly croak out the words.

Skye handed me a cup of ice chips. "Suck on these. It's better than water. Water can make you barf," she added calmly.

"How's my girl?" my dad said, leaning over the other side of my bed.

The room was spinning. I tried to swallow, but it felt like a baseball was going down my throat. I must have made a face, because Skye said, "It'll get better. Really." She handed me a pad and a pen. "Here. You can write stuff down until you can talk."

I wrote down, "How come you have two heads?" and handed her the pad. She laughed. "It's the pain medication. Some fun, huh?"

My mom stroked my forehead. "The nurse told me to let her know when you woke up. I'll be right back."

"I'll put the bed up for you, honey," my dad said. He pushed a button and the bed moved until I was in a sitting position. Something about that made me laugh. I pictured a carnival ride where a flying bed kept going up and down, up and down. My father plumped up the pillows behind me. I smiled at him, or at least I thought I did. Then I spilled the ice chips all over the bed. That struck me as totally hilarious and I started to laugh again but it hurt my throat, which made tears come to my eyes.

The door to my room opened and my mom and the nurse came in. I had never seen this nurse before. She looked like her idea of fun was eating lemons.

"How are we feeling, Rosie?" the nurse boomed at me. Her voice was so loud it made me wince. I squinted and tried to read her nameplate, but the letters blurred before my eyes. She reached over and took my pulse.

"Who are you?" I asked her.

"You may call me Ms. Reynolds," she said.

"I'll tell you what I call her later," Skye said under her breath. Ms. Reynolds shot Skye a sharp look, then wrote something on my chart.

"Can we hear all right? Do we understand?" Ms. Reynolds kept barking stupid questions at me.

"Fine, fine, fine," I said, hoping that would make her go away.

"Do we feel a little funny from the pain medication? Woozy? Teary? Do loud noises hurt our ears?" she bellowed.

"Excuse me," my dad said, "but I think my daughter can hear just fine."

Way to go, Dad! I thought blearily.

"Good," said Ms. Reynolds. "We'll feel a bit strange, though, because of the pain medication."

"I already told her that," said Skye.

The nurse glared at Skye again and then wrapped the blood-pressure cuff around my upper arm and inflated it.

"Goody! Our blood pressure is just fine," she screamed.

"Oh, super goody!" Skye exclaimed.

Ms. Reynolds turned to Skye. "You are a very sick young lady. You should be *resting*." Skye rolled her eyes. Ms. Reynolds turned back to me. "We'll be checking on you again later."

Ms. Reynolds barreled toward the door, but Skye stopped her. "Excuse me, Ms., uh, Reynolds?" Skye said.

"Yes, Skye?"

"Why do you always say 'we' when it's just you talking? I thought only the Queen of England was allowed to do that."

Ms. Reynolds's mouth twitched. "Get some rest, ladies," she barked, and sailed out the door.

As soon as she was gone, Skye sat up on her knees. "Tell me she doesn't remind you of a Doberman," she said.

I giggled. I could see her point. Even my parents were trying not to laugh.

"Well, we all call her Nurse Kennels instead of Ms. Reynolds. She barks at everybody!"

That absolutely cracked me (and my parents) up. I didn't know how I'd ever face Nurse Kennels again with a straight face.

There was a timid-sounding knock on the door. I turned my head in the direction of the door, and saw that the face peering around it belonged to Julie. I was so happy to see her!

"Um, is it okay if we come in?" she asked tentatively. At that moment Becky and Allie stuck their heads in, too.

Like a flash, Nurse Kennels stomped back into

the room. "Only four guests are allowed to visit a patient at one time," she barked.

Julie's face fell.

"Hey, that one is here to visit me, aren't you?" said Skye, pointing at Becky.

Becky caught on quickly. "Right!" she said.

"So there are only four people visiting Rosie," Skye announced innocently.

"We'll take a walk anyway and let Rosie visit with her friends alone," my mom said.

Nurse Kennels pursed her lips and flounced out of the room. My friends rushed in and surrounded my bed.

"I'm so glad to see you guys!" I whispered. "This is my roommate, Skye," I added. Skye gave them a shy smile.

My friends had brought me wonderful presents. Allie handed me a plant with tiny purple flowers on it. Becky had brought an individual raspberry souffle from the Moondance. And then Julie handed me a wrapped present. "This is from all of us."

I tore off the gold wrapping paper. Inside was a black lacquered case with a beautiful pattern of gold flowers painted on it. I opened the case. There was maybe the greatest makeup kit I had ever seen. The top tray held forty tiny little eye-shadows. Underneath that a sliding tray held twenty tiny pots of lip color and lip gloss. A third tray held squares of powder and blush, as well as eyeliner pencils and mascaras.

"This is unbelievable!" I croaked. Skye slid in next to my friends and looked at my makeup kit.

"It's really great," she said enthusiastically.

"Jennifer went with us to the mall to help pick it out," Becky said. "Actually, she had seen it on sale at Winter's. Oops, maybe I shouldn't have mentioned we got it on sale."

"It's a wonderful present. I can't wait to try it out," I whispered. I winced, because even whispering hurt.

"I *told* her to write instead of talk," said Skye. "That's what I always do after surgery," she added, going back to her own bed.

"Maybe you *should* write," said Allie, handing me the pad of paper.

I wrote down, "What did you decide to do about Jennifer and the party?"

"I changed my vote," said Julie.

"Good!" I wrote.

"You were right," Julie added. "She's really okay. She said yes right away when we asked her. In fact, she's already come up with some great ideas for the party that we hadn't even thought of!"

"Great," I wrote. "Like what?"

"Hi!" came a bright-sounding voice from the door. It was Jennifer herself, looking extremely cute in a fuzzy pink sweater with rose-colored leggings and long, dangly pearl earrings. "Sorry I'm late," she said in a rush. "I had to walk Bear. Hi, Rosie!"

"Hi," I wrote. "How's Bear doing?"

"Oh, he's fine," she said.

"Great outfit," Skye said to Jennifer.

"Thanks," said Jennifer, with a friendly smile at Skye. "I'm Jennifer Peterson," she added politely.

"Skye Friedman," said Skye. She looked at me. "Boy, you have a lot of friends," she added. Having Skye say that made me feel really good. I looked around at my friends. It meant a lot to me that they had all come to visit me.

Then I started to feel a little bad about it. Skye seemed kind of lonely to me—maybe she didn't have many friends herself. I looked over to see if she was feeling left out, but she'd picked up a magazine and seemed to be reading intently.

"We were just telling Rosie about the great ideas you've come up with for Sarah's party on Saturday," Allie told Jennifer.

"I'm so glad you guys asked me to help," said Jennifer. "It's going to be so much fun!"

"Jennifer came up with the idea of having a snow-sculpting contest," Julie said.

"It's going to be great," Allie added. "Ben's going to help us pile up extra snow around the area where we're going to have the party. Then we'll divide the kids into teams and let them create snow sculptures."

"It's really nice of Ben to help us, isn't it?" Jennifer said.

"Yeah, Sarah's lucky to have such a nice big brother," Allie agreed.

Jennifer laughed. "I'm glad he's not *my* brother!" she said. "He's way too cute to have for a brother!"

Everyone laughed at that.

"It's going to be so cool," Julie said. "Some of Ben's friends are coming, too, to help with the snow sculptures."

I tried to smile at all the enthusiasm my friends were showing about the party I was going to miss. The Mardi Gras costume party. The party that would include Ben Barrow and Jennifer Peterson but not me.

"Oh, you guys, I finally thought up my costume!" Jennifer said. "I'm going to be an Indian princess."

"I'm going as Vermilion," said Allie shyly.

"Miss Laura helped me with it. She lent me all these wonderful scarves and a red sequined hat."

"Jennifer helped me make a great red yarn wig so that I can go as Raggedy Ann," said Julie. "It's really cute."

My parents came back into the room just then. I was glad, actually. I didn't want to hear any more about how terrific the party was going to be. I didn't want to hear about how much help Jennifer was or how cute she thought Ben was or what great costumes everyone had.

"I think we should let Rosie get some rest," said my mom.

"Oh, right," said Julie. "Hey, when do you leave the hospital?"

"Her doctor says Friday morning," my dad said.

"I'll call Friday, then" Julie said. "We really miss you, you know," she added.

Hearing Julie say that almost made me cry, because it didn't really seem like my friends missed me very much at all. *Maybe it's just the pain medication making me weepy,* I thought. But there they were, all excited about the party, planning their costumes and all the fun things they were going to do. It was obvious that they could do it perfectly well without me. And then there was Jennifer. Now my friends seemed to be getting along with her just fine. *Maybe they'll want her to join The Party Line permanently,* I thought. *Maybe . . . maybe she'll take my place.*

Everyone said good-bye and the room was quiet except for the sound of a soap opera that Skye was watching. I moved the makeup kit to the table next to my bed. Was it just my imagination that my friends seemed to carry on perfectly well without me? Sure, Jennifer was nice, but if it had been up to them she would still be an outsider, not a part of the group at all. Did they have to all of a sudden think she was so wonderful and had such great ideas? Even Julie seemed to really like her! And if that weren't enough, Jennifer was going to be working with Ben on the snow sculptures. What if Ben started to like her?

When Dr. Petrelli comes in later to look at my tonsils I should probably ask him to examine my head, I thought. What was I thinking? I should be happy my friends had finally really accepted Jennifer. It had been *my* idea, after all, for them to ask her to help out with the party. Just because they became better friends with Jennifer didn't mean they would start being worse friends with me. Right? Right!

So why am I feeling so weird? I asked myself. I sighed a big sigh.

"What's the prob, roomie?" Skye asked me.

"Nothing," I said, sure she wouldn't understand.

"Your friends are really nice," Skye said. "Jennifer wears such cool clothes."

Oh, great. Even Skye was in the Jennifer fan club. And to think that I had done a makeover on Jennifer to improve her looks!

"I just want to be left alone," I said to Skye, closing my eyes again. "My throat hurts," I added.

"Sure," said Skye, but she sounded hurt.

What was wrong with me? Skye had been nothing but nice to me and there I was, acting awful to her.

"It's just that, well, I guess I feel kind of left out," I said in a small voice.

"Yeah, I know the feeling," Skye said.

"You do?" I asked her.

"Sure," said Skye. "For example, my whole family is really into athletics. My sister plays varsity basketball and my brother plays varsity football. But I can't do any sports at all." She said it matter-of-factly. I nodded as she continued, "Then take school. I have to miss a lot of school. It's hard to make close friends when you spend a lot of time in the hospital."

"Yeah," I murmured, "I hadn't thought of that."

"Anyway," Skye said, "I could tell how much your friends like you. You're really lucky."

She was right. I *was* lucky. I felt like the most ungrateful person in the world.

"Not to change the subject, but—well, I was wondering if I could ask you a favor," Skye said.

"Sure," I answered.

"I thought maybe you could show me how to use some makeup, since you got that great makeup kit. I'd like to look a little better next time Dr. Jeff comes around. He thinks of me as a little kid. Can you believe it?" Skye shook her head disgustedly.

"Sure I could," I said. I studied Skye's face and hair. She had very pale, slightly freckled skin, big hazel eyes, and a cloud of curly black hair. "I'd say we go with pink tones."

"Pink? Really?" Skye asked eagerly.

"Yeah. You have beautiful, pale skin, so I don't want to use anything too gaudy."

"Right," Skye agreed, her face lighting up. "Are you feeling too crummy to do it now? I mean, before Dr. Jeff comes back to see me?"

"I'm not sure," I said. I still felt a little dizzy and strange.

"Oh, that's okay," said Skye, but her face fell a little. "Want to watch TV?" she asked me, changing the subject.

I didn't want to watch TV. What I wanted was to be with Julie and Becky and Allie that very minute. I wanted to be planning Sarah's Mardi Gras party. The more I thought about it, the more depressed I got.

"Ice cream!" Angela, the nurse's aide, sang out as she entered our room. "It's the best thing about getting your tonsils out," she said to me. "Hope you like chocolate."

"Sure," I said listlessly. She put the chocolate ice cream down on the tray next to my bed.

"You want some apple juice, Skye?" Angela asked her.

"Spare me," said Skye, rolling her eyes.

"Well, let me know if you change your mind," Angela said as she walked out the door.

I was too depressed even to care about chocolate ice cream. "You can have my ice cream, Skye," I offered.

She made a face. "It's that crappy hospital ice cream. Definitely inferior quality," she pronounced. "Now, Aunt Jessica has the high-grade stuff. Want me to call her and ask her to bring you some?" she asked.

"Only if you want some," I said.

"Can't. I'm on liquids for twenty-four hours. My surgery is tomorrow morning."

I turned to look at her. "Really? You never said anything."

Skye shrugged. "No biggie. I'm used to it."

"You're not scared?" I could hardly believe that I'd been so petrified about my minor little tonsillectomy when Skye was being really cool about her heart operation.

Skye was quiet for a second. "Maybe just a little," she finally said. "But it isn't worth thinking about it."

I realized that I had been completely wrapped up in my own problems while Skye, who had much bigger problems, tried to make me feel better. That didn't make me feel like a very nice person.

"Hey, Skye," I said, "I'm really starting to feel better. How about if we do your makeover now?"

"Really?" she asked me excitedly.

"Sure," I answered, "if you don't mind coming over to my bed. I still feel a little wobbly."

Skye bounced off her bed and planted herself cross-legged at the foot of mine. "Okay," she said, closing her eyes. "I'm in your hands."

I opened my new makeup kit and pulled out the tray of eyeshadows. I chose a deep rosy beige shade and brushed it across her eyelids. Then I used a gray pencil and made a tiny line underneath her lower eyelashes. I smudged the line with an applicator so that it was just a soft shadow, making her eyes seem even bigger and more luminous. I swirled some clear mascara on her eyelashes. Then I chose a pink blush and brushed it on her cheekbones. I finished with a pale strawberry-colored lip gloss.

"I can't wait to see this," Skye said, jumping off my bed and heading for the mirror in the bathroom. "Wow," she said when she saw her face. "I must look at least fifteen now, don't you think?"

"At least," I agreed with her.

"What about my hair?" she asked. "I hate it. It's too bushy."

"How about if we put the front of it back in a braid?" I suggested. "Then it will be nice and fluffy in back and sleek in front." Skye sat on my bed again and I braided the front of her hair. With her hair off her face you could appreciate her delicate bone structure. I scrutinized the finished makeover. "You look great," I decided.

Skye ran back into the bathroom to look at her hair. "I love it!" she squealed. "I'm never washing my face! And I'm never brushing my hair. Oh, I know!" she said, her eyes alight. "Take my picture like this!"

"You have a camera here?" I asked her. It seemed strange to bring a camera to a hospital.

"Sure," Skye said. "I always bring my camera. I like to catch the nurses doing funny things. You should see some of the winners I've got of old Kennels herself! Also, I like to keep a scrapbook of my roommates."

Skye pulled a camera out of the small bag by her bed. "Here," she said, handing me the camera. "Just push this little button. It focuses and everything all by itself." She looked around, deciding where to pose. "What if I stand by the door?" she suggested.

"Okay," I said, aiming the camera at her.

"No, wait. Let me stand closer to you." Skye moved in closer to my bed. "Now no one will be able to tell it's a hospital room," she explained. "I could have been on vacation somewhere, and a really cute guy could have snapped my picture in the hotel lobby." Skye smiled brightly and I took the photo.

"Thanks," she said. "You're the best roommate I've had yet." Skye went over to her bed and lay down. "Whew. I guess I *am* a little tired." She closed her eyes.

"Good luck tomorrow," I whispered to her.

Skye smiled without opening her eyes. "Piece of cake," she murmured. "Thanks, roomie. That photo's gonna be awesome."

"Awesome," I agreed, and watched Skye until she was fast asleep.

Eight

It was about dawn the next morning when something woke me up. In the half-light I could see Skye standing at the window.

"Are you all right?" I whispered to her.

She didn't answer right away. Then she said, "Did you ever notice how pretty the world is before everyone is up? It seems like anything is possible, like wonderful, exciting things could happen to you."

I didn't say anything, because I didn't know what to say. She looked out the window for a while longer. "I'm kind of scared," she whispered in the tiniest of voices.

"It's okay to be scared, Skye."

She turned to me and gave me a small smile. "Yeah. Well, I'm not big on admitting it, if you know what I mean. Like, I always try to act really brave in front of the parental units, so they won't get too upset. Sometimes it's exhausting," she confessed.

"It would probably be okay to tell them the truth," I ventured.

Skye didn't say anything. Then she took a deep breath and seemed to shake off her dark mood. "Hey, let's get some good photos before they show up and give me the la-la land shot." She handed me the camera and posed on her bed like a sexy movie star—except she was still wearing her funny Elvis shirt and big gym socks. "Whaddya think?"

I giggled and took her picture. We took pictures of each other as the dawn broke outside our window. Before we knew it, Dr. Jeff had arrived.

"Morning, girls," he said. "How's my favorite patient?" he asked Skye.

"Glad you stopped by," Skye said breezily. You'd never have known she was the same scared girl I had seen earlier.

"Your parents are on their way in," Dr. Jeff said.

"Oh, no," Skye said hastily. "I'll see them after."

"Are you sure, Skye?" Dr. Jeff said.

"I'm sure. They'll be all scared and stuff. You know how parental units are."

"Okay," Dr. Jeff said quietly.

"Hey, Dr. Jeff, while you're here, why don't you

make yourself useful and take a picture of me with Rosie?"

Skye came over to my bed and draped her arm around my shoulders. "Say sex!" she shouted gaily as Dr. Jeff snapped our photo.

Angela came in to give Skye her shot.

"I'm off to la-la land, everyone!" I heard Skye say from behind the curtain drawn around her bed.

I stuck my head in when the coast was clear. "I know you'll be fine," I said encouragingly.

The shot was already starting to take effect. Skye's eyes were drooping closed. "I'll get you a copy of the photo," she said.

I watched as Skye was wheeled away to surgery. I couldn't believe how brave she was.

Dr. Petrelli had told me I would be able to leave the next morning, so I probably wouldn't see Skye before I left. I decided to do something special for her. I got out my pencils and sketch pad and spent the rest of the evening drawing her a get-well card. I drew Skye playing baseball, and put a good-looking guy who sort of resembled Dr. Jeff in the stands, cheering her on. I left it on the table by her bed, where I was sure she'd see it.

The next morning my dad drove me home. I was so happy to get out of the hospital! When I walked upstairs to my room I found that my parents had filled it with bright flowers.

"Welcome home, Rosie!" my dad said.

"It's beautiful," I said.

"You feel like resting, sweetie?" he asked me.

I had a plan. It had come into my head the night before. I figured if I acted really healthy and energetic, then maybe, just maybe, my parents would let me go to the party the next day. So even though I actually felt a little tired and my throat still hurt, I said, "I feel terrific!" and gave my father my brightest smile.

"Well, good," he said. "Mom made a batch of your favorite soup, mushroom-barley, before she went to work. Want some?"

"Sure!" I said, ready to bound down the stairs to prove how totally healthy I was.

"I'll bring it up," my dad said, stopping me at the door.

"You don't have to," I said. "I don't feel sick or anything."

"In bed, Miss Torres," he said. "I'm bringing up the soup."

When my parents call me "Miss Torres," I know they're serious. I sat down on the bed. "I'm *on* it, but I'm not getting *in* it," I said in a last-ditch attempt to avoid being treated like a patient.

"Don't get technical," Dad said, and went downstairs to get the soup.

I looked at the clock. It was eleven A.M., which meant that Julie, Becky, Allie, and Jennifer were in Ms. Pernell's biology class. I pictured them writing notes to one another behind their biology books. The notes would be all about the party plans. I sighed and put a Vermilion cassette into my Walkman. But the music only reminded me that Allie was planning to go to the party the next day dressed as Vermilion.

I ate the soup my dad brought up and then ended up sleeping for a couple of hours. I was really mad at myself when I woke up. I knew an afternoon nap was not the way to get my dad to appreciate that I was perfectly healthy and capable of going to the party the next day.

I could hardly wait until three-thirty, when I knew Julie would be home from school and I could talk to her. When I was sure she was back I dialed the Bergers' number. Julie's sister Heather answered the phone.

"Hello?"

"Hi, Heather. It's Rosie. Is Julie home yet?"

"Oh, hi, Rosie. How are you feeling? Julie told me you had your tonsils out."

"Fine. Couldn't be better!" I assured her.

"Really?" Heather asked me. "When I had my

tonsils out, my throat killed me for days afterward."

"Nope. Not me," I said, which was actually a lie. My throat did still hurt, but I was not going to admit that to anyone. "So, is Julie home?"

"I don't think so. Let me check. Hey, Laurel, is Julie home?" Heather yelled.

"Laurel says she went straight to Jennifer's house after school," Heather told me. "Maybe you could try her there," she suggested.

"Oh, well, I'll catch her later," I said casually. So Julie was at Jennifer's house! Probably Allie and Becky were there, too. The new foursome. Julie hadn't even come over to visit me after school. She hadn't even bothered to call. She was too busy making plans with Jennifer!

Tears came to my eyes, but I brushed them away. I couldn't let this happen. I had to prove how healthy I was, because I just *had* to go to that party!

I got out my new makeup kit and quickly brushed on some blush. Then I changed into some jeans and a bright pink cotton shirt that I figured would make my skin look radiant and healthy. I bounded downstairs, where my father and mother were having a cup of coffee.

"Hi, Mom!"

"Hi, yourself," she said. "How do you feel?"

"I feel great. Really great! Wow, I never knew I'd recuperate this quickly. It's amazing. Isn't it amazing?" I asked, looking back and forth between my parents.

"Amazing," my mom said, giving me the once-over. "What are you up to?"

"Me?" I asked with my most innocent look. "I'm not up to anything. I'm just feeling good, that's all."

My dad looked at me as if he wasn't sure what was going on, but I maintained my most angelic face. My mom shrugged. "Just take it easy for a couple of days, kiddo. No marathons," she said with a smile.

"Yeah, I won't start running again for a few days," I agreed. I like to jog every other day so I stay in shape. "I mean, I could run if I had to or something," I added. "I feel healthy enough."

"That's nice," my mom said, taking a sip of coffee. "By the way, honey, you were right about that denim jacket with the leather fringe," she said. "It sold like hotcakes." Sometimes I make suggestions to my mom about clothes for her boutique. She respects my opinion, and that makes me feel great.

"You know, Mom, Dad, I really feel like taking a walk. Don't you think that's a good idea? For me to get a little fresh air and exercise?"

"Rosie, it's freezing out. I don't think it's a good idea at all," Dad said.

"But I was thinking that if I took a walk today—just a short one—and if I felt fine afterward, well, think how much better I'd feel by tomorrow—"

"Hold it right there, Rosie," my mom said. "The light dawns. I can see where this is leading."

"You can?" I asked her, trying to look completely innocent.

"Yes, I can. I know how much you want to go to that party, honey."

"It's really important, Mom."

"I know. But doctor's orders are doctor's orders."

"Who do you think knows me better, Dr. Petrelli or you?" I asked her.

"Personally, me. Medically, Dr. Petrelli. He said no and the answer is no."

"But—" I began.

"No, buts, Rosie. Please."

I stomped back upstairs to my room, feeling completely defeated. I pictured everyone over at Jennifer's, laughing and eating junk food and planning the party. I was sure no one was missing me at all.

Nine

Saturday morning I opened my eyes to the sun shining brightly through my bedroom window, reflecting off the snow that covered the ground from the overnight snowfall. *What a great day for the party,* I thought. *Too bad I won't be there to appreciate it.*

I lay back in bed and covered my face with my quilt. Maybe I could just sleep through the entire day and pretend it never happened. I pictured Julie, Becky, Allie, and Jennifer getting ready for the party. Probably they were all over at Becky's in the attic, our special place, getting into their costumes together: my three best friends and Jennifer Peterson, all having a terrific time. Life just wasn't fair.

From underneath the covers I heard the muffled ring of the telephone. I heard my dad's footsteps and then the sound of my door being opened.

"Rosie? You awake? Julie's on the phone."

"I'm awake," I said, and scrambled out of bed. I picked up the phone in the upstairs hall.

"Hello?"

"Hi, Rosie! We're all here at Becky's. We wanted to call and see how you're feeling."

Oh, sure, I thought. *You could have called me last night, but you were too busy hanging out with Jennifer Peterson.*

"I'm okay," I said coolly.

"You don't sound okay. You sound funny," Julie said. "Hey, I called you last night, but you were already asleep. Your mom didn't want to wake you," she added.

"You did?" Instantly I felt better.

"Of course I did, you bozo."

I could hear everyone else's voices in the background. Then I heard them laughing. "Here," said Julie. "Jennifer wants to talk to you."

"Hi, Rosie," said Jennifer. "We really wish you were here."

I bet, I thought.

"It would be a lot more fun with you," she added.

"Thanks," I managed to say.

Jennifer laughed. "You should see how funny Julie looks in her Raggedy Ann wig. It's a riot!"

Becky grabbed the phone. "We all miss you," she said.

"We do!" Allie chimed in from the background.

"Thanks," I said over the big lump that was forming in my throat.

Julie got back on the phone. "Listen, we have to run, we've got a million things to do. We can't wait till you get better. Bye!"

I hung up the phone and felt tears glistening on my eyelashes.

"What's up?" my dad asked as he walked by me in the hall. He looked closely at my face. "Are you feeling sick, honey?"

"It's just not fair, Dad. I feel fine, I really do. Why can't I go to the party this afternoon?"

"You know what the doctor said," he reminded me.

I sighed.

Dad hugged my shoulders. "It's only a party. There'll be more." But it wasn't just any party. My parents didn't understand. This party was *special*. Ben Barrow would be at this party! Probably he'd skate with Jennifer, who would look so adorable all dressed up as an Indian princess.

I went back to my room and decided to cheer myself up by giving myself a manicure. I like my nails to look perfect. In fact, I often wear the press-on kind. I think they make my hands look sort of glamorous. I took off the old polish and then put on a base coat and two coats of a new color called

Poppy Pink. I was waving my hands around to help the polish dry when my parents came into my bedroom.

"We'd like to talk to you," my mom said, sitting on the edge of my bed.

At first I tried to think what I could have done wrong to make them look so serious.

"Your mother and I discussed the party you were supposed to go to today. We know how much it means to you," my dad said.

"So I called Dr. Petrelli," my mom continued. "I told him you felt fine and weren't running any fever. I asked him if it could hurt you to go to the party for a very short time—"

"Oh, Mom!" I breathed, hardly believing what I was hearing.

"A very, *very* short time," she continued firmly. "He said if you bundled up very warm and went for only a half-hour, it would be all right."

I jumped up and threw my arms around first my mom and then my dad. "You two are the best, absolutely the best parents in the whole, entire world!"

"Remember that next time I ask you to vacuum," my mom said with a grin.

"I'll drive you over there," my dad said.

"Oh, no—" I started to protest.

"I mean it," Dad said. "That way I'll be sure you only stay a few minutes."

"But that will be so humiliating, having you wait for me in the car."

My father shook his head, but he had a smile on his face. "I'll park where no one can see me, okay?"

"Okay," I said with a sigh. I wasn't in any position to argue.

Suddenly it hit me. I'd need a costume! What could I possibly throw together in time that would be fabulous? But before I figured out a costume I had to call Becky's house and tell my friends that I'd be there after all, if only for a brief appearance.

I ran to the phone and quickly dialed Becky's number. Her brother, David, answered the phone.

"Hi, David. It's Rosie. Is everyone still up in the attic?" I asked him.

"Nah, they all left a while ago. Mom drove them to the park."

"Oh. Too bad," I said.

"Actually, I'm going over there later myself. I told Ben Barrow I'd help him do this snow-sculpture thing. You want me to give them any message from you?"

I couldn't believe it! Becky's older brother, David, was actually going to help at one of our parties? David is fifteen and seriously cute, although no one is cuter than Ben. I hadn't even known he and Ben were friends.

Then a brilliant idea struck me. I wouldn't tell David to tell my friends that I'd be showing up. I'd just surprise them!

"No. Thanks anyway," I told David, hanging up the phone.

Wait . . . I had an even better idea than just surprising them by showing up. What if I showed up as a beautiful, mysterious stranger? Then I'd be able to see if they really missed me, and I'd be able to see if Ben Barrow liked Jennifer. What I needed was a wicked cool costume, something so fabulous—and such a perfect disguise—that even my very best friends wouldn't recognize me.

I tore open my closet and studied my wardrobe. What could I possibly wear? Nothing came to mind. Then for some reason I remembered the Mardi Gras display we had seen at the party store. In it had been the picture of a beautiful, mysterious-looking gypsy. That was it—I'd put together a gypsy outfit.

First things first. I didn't want to freeze, so I pulled on two pairs of black tights, one on top of the other. Then I put on a long-sleeved leotard. Over that I pulled on a bright red unitard that I sometimes wear for running. It's all one piece and fits skintight to the body. I pulled on a pair of red leg warmers over the unitard. What could I use as a gypsy skirt? I whirled around, trying to figure something out. Then I saw the multicolored, fringed shawl that covered the small table in my room. It was perfect. I made a triangle out of the scarf and tied two ends together at my waist, forming a fringed skirt open on one side. Then I pulled on a black turtleneck. So far, so good. All that I needed was a way to disguise my face. But what?

I opened my scarf drawer and pulled out a bunch of scarves. Maybe that would do it. I knotted together a bunch of small ones and draped them around my hair like a gypsy head scarf, letting them trail over one side of my face and down over my outfit. I checked my image in the mirror.

My hair was completely covered, and the sheer scarves floated around my shoulders. I thought my hair was the thing that would make me most recognizable to my friends, so the hardest part was over.

I sat down at my vanity table and studied my face. How should I make myself up to look like a gypsy? Usually my makeup is very light and natural-looking. I decided that as a gypsy I would wear much more intense makeup. (It would also help disguise me in front of my friends.) I took a black eyeliner pencil and made a thin line underneath my eyes. Then I used the shimmery gold eyeshadow from my new makeup kit, brushing it lightly on my eyelids all the way to my eyebrows. I studied the effect. Dazzling! Three coats of midnight black mascara completed my eye makeup. I used one of the little brushes that came with the kit and brushed a deep terra-cotta blush underneath my cheekbones. The final touch was bright red lipstick, something I never wear in real life. I stood up and let the multicolored scarves fall back across my face. I definitely looked like a mysterious woman.

My mom looked at me from the doorway. "You're amazing, Rosie. You created that costume in about twenty minutes!" she said.

"Does it look okay?" I asked her, twirling around.

"It's fabulous. All you need is a crystal ball," she said with a laugh. "Oh, wait, I don't have a crystal ball but I do have something great for your costume. Be right back."

I practiced soulful gypsy looks in the mirror until my mom came back.

"Here," she said, handing me a pair of huge gold hoop earrings. "These will add the final touch."

"Wow, these are great. I didn't know they made

hoops this big. Where did you get them?" I asked her. "I've never seen you wear them."

"A frightening thought," my mom said with a laugh. "They're as big as my head."

I put the hoops in my ears. "They're light-weight, though," I said, shaking my head to feel them. "Really, Mom, where did you get these?"

"Your Aunt Maria bought them for me for Christmas last year. You know your aunt—these are her idea of understated elegance. I kept them so that I could wear them when we see her. I didn't want to hurt her feelings."

"Well, they're great for my gypsy costume," I said.

My dad came into my room, jangling his car keys. "Hey, you look terrific," he said.

"Thanks, Dad," I said with a grin.

"Is Madam Gypsy ready for her caravan?" he asked me.

I pulled one chiffon scarf over the lower half of my face and wiggled my eyebrows at him. "Madam Gypsy ees ready," I said. "Pleeze, do not tell my public I am out and about. Zey beg too much for ze autographs."

My mom looked at my dad and my dad looked at my mom.

"Rosie, you are one in a million," my mom said. "Have fun."

My dad took the usual route to the park, down Montpelier Street. When we got close to the ice-skating rink, I looked at him. But before I could say anything, he said, "I know, I know, you want me to go to the back parking lot so no one sees us, right?"

I grinned at him. "Thanks, Dad."

We turned the corner and pulled into the back parking lot. "Remember, Rosie, thirty minutes and that's it."

"But if I feel all right then—"

"No," my dad said firmly.

"Okay, thirty minutes," I sighed, "but don't start counting until I actually get there."

I went around the back way until I came to the clearing and could see the rink. From a distance all I could see was a whole bunch of kids in brightly colored costumes skating around on the ice. I looked off to one side of the rink, and there were Ben Barrow, David Bartlett, and another guy I didn't know shoveling snow into huge mounds. I picked out Julie in her bright red yarn wig. Even from a distance I could see how cute she looked as Raggedy Ann. She wore red tights and a red turtleneck underneath a short white-and-blue pinafore. Becky was dressed as a traditional Japanese lady; she wore a red silk kimono that I guessed Ms. Laura had loaned her, with a black wig and lots of white face makeup. (I hoped she had a lot of layers on underneath that kimono, or else she would freeze to death!) Allie looked fantastic dressed as Vermillion. I saw Jennifer, too. She was standing with Allie, setting out food on a picnic table. Becky was helping a little girl get her skates on.

I really wanted to get a better look at the action without being seen. I noticed a large evergreen tree closer to the ice. I scurried over to the tree, sliding a bit on the snow. Fortunately everyone was too busy to notice me. From behind the tree, I could just barely hear the conversation between Allie and Jennifer as they set out the food.

"Do you think I should pour the hot chocolate?" Jennifer asked Allie.

"No, not yet. It'll get cold too fast."

Allie pulled some Mardi Gras noisemakers out of a bag and set them on the table. Julie came over to help her.

"Let's put the noisemakers in a big pile," Julie suggested. "That'll look colorful."

Allie dumped the noisemakers in the center of the picnic table. "I don't know," she sighed, "it seems like something's missing."

"I know what's missing," said Julie. "It's Rosie. She would have done some sort of amazing center-piece."

"Yeah, you're right," Allie agreed.

"Nothing is as much fun without Rosie," Julie said as she tried to arrange the noisemakers.

Just then Ben Barrow came over to the table. I ducked farther behind the tree, wanting to make absolutely certain that he couldn't see me. I peeked between the branches.

"Can I snitch some hot chocolate?" he asked Julie. "My hands are freezing from all that snow."

"Sure," said Julie, pouring some into a paper cup.

Jennifer came back over to the picnic table and smiled at Ben. I had to admit she really did look cute in her Indian princess outfit.

"Hey, that's a cute outfit," Ben said to Jennifer.

"Thanks," she said. Was it just my hyperactive (and, I'm sorry to admit, jealous) imagination, or was she giving him an extra-bright smile? "Thanks for helping us," she added. "The snow-sculpting contest will be great."

"No prob," he answered, sipping the hot chocolate.

Was Ben being polite or did he like Jennifer? How could I tell? I was really happy to hear my friends talking about how much they missed me. Now if I could only be certain that Ben wasn't interested in Jennifer!

I knew it was time to do something dramatic. I

looked at my watch. I had only another fifteen minutes before my dad would get out of the car and come after me, which would be a fate worse than death as far as I was concerned.

I crouched behind the tree, quickly took off my boots, and laced myself into my ice skates. I adjusted the chiffon scarves over my face so only my eyes and part of my forehead showed, took a deep breath, and headed for the ice.

Ten

I'm not very good at cleaning my room, I can't carry a tune, my piano playing is sometimes more mistakes than music, and my idea of cooking is dumping canned sauce on spaghetti, but I'm a great ice skater.

I hit the ice and skated around the outside edge of the rink, working up some speed. A Vermilion tape was playing over the sound system and I adjusted my strides to the rhythm. Once I hit full speed I raised one leg into an arabesque, holding my arms out gracefully. The fringe on my gypsy skirt shimmered against my unitard.

After another circuit around the ice, I peeked over my shoulder. Everyone was looking at me, even Ben Barrow! *You haven't seen anything yet,* I said to myself. I took three big, power-strides and lifted off the ice into a double axle, just the way I'd learned when I took skating lessons. It was perfect! I felt like I was flying!

As I sped past the group near the picnic bench, I heard Ben say, "Who is that?" just like he was looking at a movie star. And I *felt* like a movie star—beautiful, mysterious, and at least sixteen.

I got ready for my grand finale. The most difficult move I had ever learned was a double jump. Unfortunately, I usually can manage only one and a half jumps. But as I skated around, feeling fantastic, somehow I just knew I could do a perfect double jump. I felt the power in my legs as I lifted off the ice, turned once, twice, and landed gracefully back on the ice. I had done it!

Even nature was on my side. It was a brilliantly sunny day, and the glare on the snow was so intense that everyone was shielding their eyes, trying to get a better look at me. I could tell they didn't know who I was. I heard one little girl say "Wow" with total awe in her voice. Another little girl turned to Julie and said, "Is she an ice princess?" It was maybe the greatest moment of my life.

Once more I spun around the ice, then I jumped off on the far side of the rink, away from where everyone was standing. Quickly I ran behind the evergreen tree, unlacing my skates as fast as I could. Would I be able to make a clean getaway?

Once again, luck was with me. I watched everyone through the branches as I unlaced my skates.

Just as Ben Barrow was about to walk toward my hiding place, his little sister, Sarah, fell down on the ice. Her brother immediately went over to make sure she was all right, while I threw my skates over my shoulder and ran back to the car. Success!

I jumped into the car and slammed the door.

"Okay, let's go!" I said to my dad.

He lowered the newspaper he had been reading and started to fold it in a maddeningly slow manner. I wasn't sure no one had seen me head toward the parking lot, so I wanted to get out of there as quickly as possible.

My dad started the car and backed out of the parking space. "Well, did you have fun?"

"It was absolutely great!" I said, still breathless from skating.

My dad looked at me as he turned onto Montpelier Street. "Those pink cheeks are from skating and not from a fever, I presume?" He lifted one hand off the steering wheel and felt my forehead.

"Oh, I don't feel sick at all," I reassured him. "In fact, I feel absolutely wonderful!"

"Glad to hear it," my dad said.

I played over the scene in my mind. Everything had gone perfectly! My favorite part was when Ben had stared at me and said, "Who is that?" like I was Vermilion or something! He had been looking at me, Rosie, mysterious ice princess and gypsy queen of Mardi Gras—and he didn't even know it!

I ran into the house and looked for my mother, because I wanted to tell her what had happened. My mother loves a good joke. Unfortunately she had gone over to Cinderella, so I'd have to wait to tell her.

I went up to my room and looked at myself in the mirror. "Rosie," I said out loud to my reflection, "you are ze most wonderful gypsy in ze world." I stared dreamily at my reflection, remembering Ben's face as he had watched me spinning on the ice.

"Rosie, your mom just called to see how you were doing," my dad said from the doorway.

"I'm fine," I said to him.

"That's what I told her. She said she'll be home in an hour."

"Okay," I said dreamily.

"She said you should catch up on your homework," Dad said, walking away.

Oh, really! Silly father. Doesn't he know? Beautiful gypsy queens don't have to worry about dull things like homework. They're much too busy being glamorous and making great-looking guys like Ben Barrow fall at their feet.

Eleven

I remember feeling a little sleepy as I took off my gypsy costume. The next thing I knew I was waking up. It was already dark out, and my mom was sitting on the edge of my bed.

"What time is it?" I asked, still fuzzy.

"Five o'clock. Did you have fun?"

I sat up, instantly wide awake. "Oh, Mom, it was the greatest! Really!"

"That's great, Rosie," my mom said. "I bet your friends were glad to see you."

"Actually, Mom . . . Can you keep a secret?"

"Of course I can," she said with a laugh.

I leaned forward in bed. "Well, listen to this. I skated around really fast, did all these neat skating tricks, and no one knew it was me! Not even Julie! That's how great my disguise was!"

"Really?" my mom said. "Not even Julie?"

"Really! It was awesome. I was the mystery woman."

My mother laughed and hugged me.

"How is the mystery woman feeling after all that excitement?" my mom asked me.

"Great," I said, hugging my pillow, "just great."

I heard noise downstairs and within seconds Julie, Becky, Allie, and Jennifer were crowding into my bedroom.

"Hi, you guys!" I practically screamed.

"Hi, yourself," said Julie. "We wanted to see you in person and tell you about the party."

"It was great fun but I'm pooped," Becky said, falling back on one of my giant floor pillows.

"Me, too," Allie said. "I never knew skating could be such hard work."

Julie laughed. "It's not skating that's hard work. It's a Mardi Gras skating party for fifth graders that's so exhausting!"

"It was so much fun," Jennifer added shyly. "I really want to thank you guys for including me."

"We should thank you," Becky said. "You really worked hard, and we couldn't have done it without you."

"So, was it terrific or what?" I asked them.

"It was great," Julie said. "Hey, you'll never believe what happened," she went on excitedly.

My mom caught my eye. "I, uh, think I'll go get you girls some cookies," she said, disappearing fast.

"So what happened?" I asked Julie.

Julie sat down on my bed. "Well, it was pretty early. The kids were just starting to skate, and from out of nowhere this beautiful girl appears!"

"Really?" I squeaked.

"Really!" Becky confirmed. "It was amazing. She seemed to have come out of thin air. And she was dressed in this great gypsy outfit!"

"Anyway," Julie continued, "she glided out onto the ice, and she had all these gauzy scarves swirling around her, so we couldn't really see exactly what she looked like."

My mom walked back into the room with a plate of chocolate chip cookies. Julie dove for them immediately. "Thanks, Mrs. Torres. I'm starved!" she said.

"Your parents will probably kill me for ruining your appetites," my mom said.

"Oh, don't worry," Julie said, happily munching away. "Nothing ruins my appetite."

"That I know," my mom told her. "Have fun!" she said to all of us as she left.

"So tell me more about this girl," I said.

"Well," said Julie, "she did some fancy skating moves, and the little kids sort of moved back to watch her."

"They were all fascinated," Allie added.

"Right," Julie said. "Then she did this perfect double axle. I mean, perfect!"

"And if that weren't incredible enough, she finished with a double jump," Jennifer said. "I was so amazed. I can't even do a double jump and I had years of skating lessons back in Minnesota."

"The only one I know who even comes close is you, Rosie," Julie said, "and no offense, but this girl was an even better skater than you are."

"Really?" I pretended to be impressed. I was dying, absolutely dying to tell them the truth, but I was having way too much fun.

Becky reached for a cookie. "So then I heard Ben say, 'who is that?' But no one knew."

"So then Ben said, 'I've got to find out who that girl is. She's awesome!'" Julie went on. "But just as he was about run after her, Sarah fell down on the ice and he went to make sure she was okay. By the time he turned around again, the girl was gone!"

"Vanished," Allie added, her eyes wide.

"Disappeared!" said Becky.

"Wow," I breathed.

"The whole rest of the afternoon Ben kept asking everyone if they knew who she was," Julie said. "Oh, gee, Rosie, I hope that doesn't hurt your feelings," she added quickly.

"No, it's okay," I told her solemnly. "I'm just sorry I missed all the excitement."

"It doesn't necessarily mean that he likes her, Rosie. I mean, he doesn't even know her."

"Julie, I said it's okay!"

"She might be a really obnoxious person or something. She might be—"

I held up my hand. "Really, Julie. It's no problem. I can handle the competition."

Julie raised her eyebrows. "Well, aren't *you* the cool woman of the world!"

"I just have self-confidence, that's all," I said airily.

"Still," said Julie, "mystery woman or no mystery woman, the party really wasn't the same without you."

"How are you feeling, anyway?" Allie asked.

"Much better," I said. "Much, much better." I could barely keep the laughter out of my voice.

"What's so funny?" Julie asked. "Do you have a fever or something? You're acting kind of strange."

"No, I'm fine," I managed to say, but then I cracked up. "Um, I'm just laughing at the story you told me about the mystery skater. It must have been really funny."

"Speaking of funny," Becky said, "my mom will not be amused if I don't get home for dinner."

"Maybe you guys can eat here," I said. "Wait a minute while I go ask, okay?" I raced downstairs and found my mother stirring a huge pot on the stove.

"Mom, this is such a riot!" I whispered. "They just told me all about this beautiful girl who showed up dressed as a gypsy and how she amazed everyone! I can't believe I pulled it off!"

"I can't believe you did, either. When do you let them in on the joke?" my mom asked.

"Soon," I told her. "But this is so much fun, I just want to make it last a little longer."

My mother raised her eyebrows but said nothing.

"That stew looks great," I said, changing the subject. "I notice you really have a lot there."

"Well, no one makes a small pot of stew," my mom said.

"I was wondering, since we've got plenty, could my friends stay for dinner?"

"Sure," said my mom.

"Great. I'll go ask them," I said, giving her a peck on the cheek. "Thanks, Mom."

"Hey," I said when I got back upstairs, "call your parental units. You all can stay for dinner."

I couldn't use the term 'parental units' without thinking of Skye. I hadn't even called her yet to see how she was. After my friends had all called their parents and gone downstairs to help my mother set the table, I dialed the hospital and asked for my old room.

Her Aunt Jessica answered and remembered me right away.

"Hi, Rosie. How's your throat feeling these days?" she asked.

"Pretty good," I told her. "How's Skye?"

Jessica sighed. "Well, this last surgery was really tough on her. She's pretty weak. But she came through it with flying colors."

"I was wondering, could I come and visit her?" I asked.

"Oh, she'd love that, Rosie! She said you were the best roommate she ever had!"

"Will she still be in the hospital tomorrow or the next day?"

"She'll be in the hospital for quite a few tomorrows," Jessica said.

"Oh," I said. I didn't know what else to say.

"But listen," Jessica told me, "she loves company when she's recuperating. You know Skye—so much energy!"

"Would you give Skye my phone number?" I said. "That way she can call me if she wants to. I'll try to visit her real soon." I gave Jessica my number before we said goodbye.

When I got downstairs Julie was just bringing

the last steaming bowl of beef stew over to the table.

"Smells great," I said, sitting down. "Hey, remember Skye, my roommate at the hospital?"

"She seemed pretty neat," Julie said.

"I think I may visit her tomorrow. She had heart surgery."

"Heart surgery," Allie said with a shudder. "That sounds serious."

"I guess," I said. "She's had lots of surgeries, she told me. I just feel bad for her, stuck in the hospital so long. I thought maybe you guys would come with me and help cheer her up."

"I'd go," said Becky, "but we have a Party Line meeting tomorrow. You'll be able to come, won't you, Rosie?"

"Of course!" I said.

"Hang on a minute, Rosie," my mom said. "It depends."

"On what?" I asked. "I feel fine, Mom. Really."

"Dr. Petrelli said you might run a low-grade fever for a few days. We'll take your temperature tonight and see."

"I don't have a fever," I said.

"Good," my mom said, "then you won't mind if I take your temperature. Anyone want seconds?" Julie was the first one to respond to that, naturally.

Allie was staring dreamily down at her empty plate. "I keep wondering about the mystery skater who showed up today. Maybe she was a famous movie star in disguise."

"She sure was a great skater," Becky said. "What's really funny, Rosie, is that some of the kids actually thought she was part of the party! They thought *we'd* planned the whole thing!"

"Really?" I asked.

"Really!" Julie said.

"It was so romantic," Allie said. "A beautiful girl shows up out of nowhere and then vanishes without ever letting anyone know who she is."

"I wish I could skate like that," Becky said with a sigh.

"Maybe she could teach you," I said.

"Well, that would be kind of tough, since we don't know who she is or where she came from," Julie said.

"Who knows? You might see her again soon," I said breezily. "Maybe this mysterious beauty lives closer than you think."

Twelve

I knew it was going to be bad news as soon as my mom stuck that stupid thermometer under my tongue. You know that feeling when you have just a small fever, when you feel a little sick but not sick enough not to want to go out and have fun? Well, that's how I felt. Sure enough, I was running a tiny fever.

"We probably shouldn't have let you out for that skating party," my mom said with a sigh.

"Yes, you should have," I said. "I mean, it's just a *little fever*. I feel fine. Really!"

My mom laughed and kissed my forehead. "Anyway, no Party Line meeting for you tomorrow. And definitely no trip to the hospital to see Skye."

"But—"

"Read my lips: no. You stay in all day tomorrow and we'll see how you are for Monday. If you feel okay you can go visit Skye after school on Monday."

"Great. I'll miss The Party Line meeting and then be well enough to go to school Monday morning," I grumbled. I got up to go call Julie and tell her I couldn't be at The Party Line meeting the next day.

"Oh well, the meeting won't be the same without you, but the four of us will have to carry on," Julie said when I told her.

The *four* of us? "You invited Jennifer?" I said incredulously.

"Of course we did," said Julie. "What are we supposed to do, have her share the work and not have her come to the meeting where we get paid?"

"Oh . . . no, I guess you couldn't do that," I said in a small voice.

"Hey, including her was your idea in the first place!" Julie reminded me.

"I know, I know. It's okay." I said. "I'm just sorry I can't be there, too."

"Ditto," said Julie. "Well, I'll pass the word. Feel better soon!" Julie said before she hung up.

Feel better soon. How could I feel better when I knew that Jennifer would be at The Party Line meeting and I wouldn't? What if they asked her to join permanently, since she did such a wonderful job on the Mardi Gras party? Could there be five members of The Party Line? It just wouldn't be the same!

I went back to my room. I decided to call Skye before I fell asleep. The phone number was still sitting on my dresser. I went into the hall and dialed her number.

"Hi, Skye. It's Rosie."

"Oh, hi!" She sounded kind of weak, but happy to hear me.

"How are you?" I asked.

"Fine, fine. No skydiving until tomorrow," she said.

"Would it be okay if I came to visit you Monday after school?"

"Really?"

She sounded so surprised. "Yes, really," I told her.

"Oh, it'd be great," she said. "Well, gotta go. See you Monday, okay?"

"You bet," I said. "See you." I headed for bed as soon as I'd hung up.

The next morning I woke up to see the snow falling outside my window. I put on my slippers and went downstairs to make some hot chocolate. My mom and dad were at the kitchen table reading the Sunday paper.

"Hey, look at this," my mom said, holding up the Science and Medicine section of the paper.

"Isn't this the girl you roomed with at the hospital?"

I looked at the paper. There was a picture of Skye with an article about her rare heart condition. The picture showed Skye standing in a park with her parents, smiling and looking confident. Unfortunately the caption underneath said her name was Cecilia Friedman. I knew Skye would hate that.

"Yeah, that's her," I said. I leaned over my mom's shoulder and read the article with her. It talked about how surgeons at Canfield General had used a new technique to close the hole in her heart. The doctors thought it might cure her, but said the technique was still very experimental.

"Wow," I said when I finished the article. "And she acts so upbeat, like nothing bothers her."

"She's very brave," my mom said.

"I'll say," I agreed. I felt really glad that I had done her makeup before I left the hospital, and even gladder that I was going to visit her.

"You know, Mom, I don't think she has very many friends," I said.

"All the more reason for you to make an effort," my mother said. "Because I'm sure she really appreciates it."

"Yeah," I said. The phone rang just as I was pouring my hot chocolate. "I'll get it," I said.

"Rosie! This is Skye."

Skye! It seemed eerie talking to her on the phone right after I had read about her in the newspaper. She still didn't sound like her old self, though she definitely sounded better than she had the night before.

"Hi! How are you feeling?"

"Ask me something interesting, like have I kissed Dr. Jeff yet," she said.

"Okay." I giggled. "Have you kissed Dr. Jeff yet?"

"No," she said. "But I haven't given up. Anyway, I just called to thank you for leaving that get-well card for me the other day. I was kind of out of it last night, and I forgot. It was so beautiful! Rosie, you should be a professional artist!"

"Thanks, Skye."

"So are you coming to see me tomorrow?" she said. She was trying to sound blasé, but I could tell she really wanted me to come.

"You bet! Tomorrow after school is okay, right?" I confirmed.

"Let me check my date book. Oops, sorry. Tomorrow I'm giving kissing lessons to the drummer from Bastille." She giggled.

"Well, in that case I wouldn't miss it. See you tomorrow, Skye."

"Sure," said Skye. "And Rosie?"

"Yeah?"

"Thanks," she said quietly, then hung up.

I finished my hot chocolate and wandered back upstairs. Boy, was I bored. I certainly didn't feel sick enough to have to stay in the house.

I knew it was just about time for The Party Line meeting to get started. I pictured all my friends up in the attic, laughing and talking about how great the Mardi Gras skating party had been. The party I had missed.

At least, as far as they knew, I'd missed it. That made me smile. I sure had pulled one over on them! I closed my eyes and remembered the admiring looks on everyone's face as I executed my perfect double jump. And best of all, I remembered the look on Ben's face as he watched the beautiful, mysterious skater disappear into the trees.

I decided to fool around with the gypsy look a little bit—anything to keep from being bored. First I tied the scarves the way I had the day of the party, just to see if I'd really looked as good as I remembered. (I had.)

Then I tried tying the scarves into a big, floppy bow on top of my head. It was kind of funky. After that I tried braiding some of the thinner chiffon scarves into my hair. That was a really amazing look.

Suddenly, my mom called from downstairs. "Rosie, your friends are here!"

I must have been so preoccupied, I hadn't even heard the doorbell! Like a flash, I tugged the scarves out of my hair and shoved the whole pile under my bed. My friends came bounding into my bedroom.

"What are you guys doing here?" I screamed.

"Surprise!" said Julie. "We decided that if Rosie can't come to The Party Line meeting, The Party Line meeting will come to Rosie!"

Unbelievable! My friends started unpacking big bags, and in a flash my room was filled with paper plates of potato chips and cookies, and a bowl of the Moondance's super raspberry souffle.

"This is great! You guys are too much," I said.

"Well, it just wasn't the same without you," Allie said. "We really missed you."

"Really?" I asked.

"Of course, really. You're such a bozo, Torres," Julie said.

"We have a special surprise for you, direct from Matthew," Becky said. She carefully pulled something from another bag.

It was a gorgeous cake with white frosting. "Get Better Soon," was written across the top in different colors.

"Oh, you guys are so sweet!" I said.

"Speaking of sweet," said Julie, "let's dig in!" She was kneeling down on the rug next to my bed.

"We even brought the cake knife with us," said Becky, "and the paper plates."

Julie leaned forward to watch Becky cut into the cake, and that's when her foot caught on one of the scarves under my bed.

"What is this?" Julie asked, pulling it out. All my other gypsy-disguise stuff came out with it. Oops!

"Rosie! It was *you*! *You* were the mystery skater!"

"You let us go on and on about that girl!" yelled Becky.

"And it was you all the time!" Allie finished.

"You're a great skater," Jennifer marveled.

"Can you believe I did a perfect double jump?" I asked Julie, grabbing her hands.

"What I can't believe is that you lied to us," Julie said, dropping my hands.

"What do you mean?" I asked.

"I mean that we only found out the truth by accident. Were you ever going to tell us?" Julie asked.

"Of course I was!" I said. "You know we tell each other everything."

"*I* know that," said Julie. "I just wasn't sure *you* did."

"I was going to tell you tomorrow at school," I said. "Really! I called Becky's house to tell all of you that my mom said I could come to the party for a half-hour, but you were already gone. And then I thought . . . um, I thought maybe you guys didn't miss me at all. So, I thought that if I showed up as someone else, I could find out if you really *did* miss me."

"And what did you find out?" Becky asked me.

"Well," I began quietly, "it seemed like you might have missed me a little. . . ."

"A little?" Julie broke in. "Nothing is the same without you. The party just didn't have that special Rosie touch. Even Ben Barrow asked about you."

"He did?" I asked her.

"He sure did," Jennifer said.

"I thought he was only interested in the mysterious gypsy."

"Well, her too." Julie laughed. "But before that he asked me twice where you were."

"Twice?" I asked, totally thrilled.

"*Twice*, you nut," exclaimed Julie.

"Oh, that's fabulous!" I screamed.

"Listen, Rosie, promise me you won't start keeping secrets from us," said Julie, much more serious than usual.

"I promise," I said meekly. Boy, was I beginning to feel like a big jerk! "I just wanted to make sure you guys still wanted me around."

Julie shook her head. "Is she unbelievable or what?" she asked the others. "You are my very best friend in the world, Rosie Torres, even if you do act like a total moron sometimes." Julie tried to hide her smile. "What do you say we dig into your cake now?" she asked. "Or don't mysterious gypsies eat cake?"

"Oh, they love cake," I assured her. "But I've got an idea. You remember Skye, my roommate from the hospital?"

They all nodded.

"Well, I was thinking that maybe we could all go visit her tomorrow, and we could take the cake to her. After all, it doesn't say my name on it, and we get to enjoy Matthew's cakes all the time."

"But it was a present for you," Becky objected.

"The best present I could have is having all of you bring The Party Line meeting over to my house."

Julie looked at Becky. "Is she about to get mushy?"

Becky shrugged her shoulders. "I think she already did."

Allie poured fruit punch into our paper cups.

"Here's to friendship," I said, raising my cup.

"To friendship!" they all cried.

"And to perfect double jumps, which my best friend promises to teach me," Julie added.

"You got it!" I said.

And in my head, I added one more toast. *Here's to Skye,* I thought. *Get well soon. May you find friends who will always stick by you, just like mine.* I had a feeling she'd already found one for sure. Me.

SPECIAL PARTY TIP
Rosie's Mardi Gras king cake

You don't have to live in New Orleans to enjoy king cake. In fact, you don't even have to use an authentic king cake recipe.

You can use just about any plain coffee cake recipe or instant mix to make a king cake. The most authentic recipe would be for a sweet yellow cake that's plain except for icing. There are two things that really make a king cake special. One is the terrific harlequin icing; the other is the tiny doll hidden in the cake.

The icing should be done after the cake is baked and cooled. Just take a regular white icing recipe and make enough to cover the whole top of the cake. Then divide it into three portions. Use food coloring (I like to use the all-natural kind) to color the icing one-third purple, one-third golden-yellow, and one-third green. Now ice the cake in alternating colors, so you have a few inches colored purple, then a few inches colored gold, then a few inches green and so on. You should brush the icing so it just covers the top of the cake.

If you decide to bake the baby doll in the cake, make sure the one you use won't melt in the hot oven. (Not only would this ruin your cake, but it would be gross!) The doll should be about the size of a quarter, and often is made of hard plastic. If you don't want to bake the doll inside the cake, you can always add it after the cake is baked. You can put the doll on a platter and then just plop the cake right on top of it, in which case the lucky finder will get it as soon as she takes her slice. Or you can hide the doll this way: cut a little hole out of the top of the cake and hide the doll inside. Then cover it with the bit you cut out and disguise it all with icing. (Just make sure all your party guests know about the hidden doll so no one eats it by mistake!)

The person who finds the king cake doll is king (or queen) for a day, and usually gets to wear a cardboard crown. If you're going to follow the yummy king cake custom, then the person who finds the king cake doll also gets to supply the cake for the next party!

However you do it, your king cake is sure to be a big hit!

Meet . . .

JENNIFER

by Melanie Friedman

She's the girl who's ready for anything! Especially if it's new, outrageous, and fun. Meet Willi—a perfectly normal girl whose life would be normal too—if only her best friend Jennifer wasn't absolutely crazy!

___ **#1 WHAT'S NEXT, JENNIFER?**
0-425-12603-X/$2.75

When Jennifer cooks up a plan to go get Willi a date with Robbie Wilton for the Halloween dance, her scheme backfires in a big way. Willi thinks that Robbie has fallen for Jennifer instead. Is this the end of Willi and Jennifer's friendship?

___ **#2 NO WAY, JENNIFER!**
0-425-12604-9/$2.75

Will anyone at Wellbie High still read the school news-paper's advice column, "Dear Heart," when they find out it's written by a lowly freshman? Willi writes the column and is trying to keep that a secret. But Jennifer has decided that "Dear Heart" should come out of hiding, and Willi can't stop her!